Wisdom of Les Misérables Trilogy: Book 3

Inspector Javert

at the Gates of Hell

By Alfred J. Garrotto

WLM Books

Published by WLM Books

Copyright © 2021 Alfred J. Garrotto
alfredjgarrotto.com

Printed in the United States of America
First Edition: October 2021

10 9 8 7 6 5 4 3 2 1

Garrotto, Alfred, J.
Inspector Javert at the Gates of Hell

ISBN: 978-1-950562-37-4

Cover and book design by Andrew Benzie
www.andrewbenziebooks.com

*I dedicate this book to all the amazing actors and singers
who ever played the role of Inspector Javert in movies,
on television, on stage, and in animation.
Victor Hugo must be proud of your talent
in giving flesh and voice to one of literature's
most complex characters.*

CONTENTS

FOREWORD

With publication of this third volume, I bring my Wisdom of *Les Misérables* trilogy to a close. It began in 2009, with the publication of *Lessons from the Heart of Jean Valjean* (nonfiction). At that time, I did not foresee that two more volumes, both novels, would follow, making it a perhaps hybrid trilogy. In the first volume, I offered an intimate look into my own life and the various U-turns that have made me… me.

In 2020, I gave a lot of thought to Victor Hugo's catalyst character in *Les Misérables,* Bishop Charles Francois Myriel. Hugo created a detailed outline of a book Myriel intended to write but never got around to during his active life as bishop and spiritual leader of the Diocese of Digne in southeastern France. Bravely—or foolishly—I dared to write *Bishop Myriel: In His Own Words,* completing the book he left in outline form under its intended title, *On Duty.*

Energized and on a Les Mis roll, I next set out to probe the most complex of all Hugo's characters, Inspector Javert. Early in this prison-born child's life, he followed what he deemed his divinely ordained vocation in life, to rid from the streets of France every lowlife law breaker, whether a man, woman, or child, a petty thief or the most vile, conscienceless murderer.

Climbing into the mind of Javert presented a personal problem of its own for me. Did I want this despised character crawling around inside my head every day for the year it would take to proceed from "Where have I landed?" to his final and eternal place in Afterlife? To get there, I had to ask the questions we all wonder about: What's next? What happens in that instant after my heart beats for the last time?

The easy answer to the question is, "Nothing." That may satisfy some. Those of us desiring a bit more complex answer find ourselves probing the viewpoints of religion, philosophy, or simply an internal need or hope that "something more" just has to follow. In *Inspector Javert*, I offer my own take on what happens to us when we quit the only existence we've known. I do not expect the reader to agree with my conclusion. While living in Earth Time, each of us must arrive at our own answer to the "What's next?" question, one that makes the most sense to us.

CHAPTER THE FIRST:
A LEAP INTO… WHERE?

Where have I landed?

Dizzying disorientation in this lightless place tosses me this way and that.

How did I arrive in this… this state of absolute silence?

My most recent memory?

Ah, yes, summer.

June. Of the year 1832.

Balmy post-midnight darkness.

Standing atop the concrete parapet above France's signature River Seine as it flows through the heart of Paris. Staring into a barely visible whirlpool below. Earlier events this day threw me into a state of confusion. Had I, Inspector Javert, who not once in his life entertained a second thought about any decision, allowed unaccustomed—dare I speak the word?—doubt to creep into a dark, unmapped corner of my soul?

My intention peering into the hissing abyss? To seek a ray of light as I sorted through decisions and actions of earlier this day.

Did I intend to take my own life?

Never!

Inspector Javert freely choosing suicide? Such a horror never entered the equation.

Ever.

I swear it.

What dark force, then, brought me to that isolated spot?

I needed time to repair damage to my lifelong singleness of mind.

Long ago, on a rain-soaked but to me glorious day, I swore a sacred oath to serve my country as a proud member of its police service. I considered my vow to uphold and enforce the laws of France as solemn as any monk had ever sworn to God and pope. No matter the cost. Even to surrender my life in the service of law and order.

I imagined no more honorable way to die than for my country and the security of its patriotic, law-abiding citizens.

How to explain, then, my behavior and decisions taken earlier on this fateful night, when I—when I failed in my duty to spy on a band of ragtag scoundrels who dared to revolt against the underpinnings of French society. Narrowly escaping a brush with death this night, I swore to renew my allegiance to our glorious tricolor flag and the country it heralds.

With reviving spirit and resolution, I mapped a way forward in my otherwise impeccable career.

Of a sudden, I feel—How to put it? A need to review my life, revive my dedication, reaffirm my priorities. But where to begin? I find myself... adrift... in an uncharted sea.

CHAPTER THE SECOND:
HOW IT ALL WENT WRONG

D amn that Thenardier runt! What did they call that villain's brat child? Ah yes, Gavroche. After exposing my disguise, the brat thug fell before the barricade. One of our brave army snipers felled him. Good riddance! All of Paris rests easier for his passing.

About the barricade. …Imagine! Self-aggrandizing schoolboys and ne'er do well hooligans declaring themselves divinely ordained to change the flow and right order of history. This day, France taught those rebels a lesson their kind shall not forget. They died for a single day's doomed display of youthful braggadocio.

I ask them now, "Did your sacrifice make a centime's worth of difference?" Other than to clear our streets of two score misguided and expendable riffraff.

A growling voice interrupts, *"Javert, you make yourself sound oh so clever."*

"Be still, false conscience! I had no shred of control over what happened."

"Your sole mission obliged you to assess the rebels' strength opposite your assembling forces. You went too far, invested too much personal pride in your assigned task."

Guilty as charged.

Even worse. After discovering my lifelong nemesis Jean Valjean's presence among the rebel band, I veered from my mission. In my defense I argue, "Unexpected events write their own pages in the history of the world." A weak response I admit, for one as experienced as I.

*　　　*　　　*

Now I find myself in this unknown place—this mysterious state of dark awareness.

Waiting. But for what?

Reprieve?

Justification?

Reincarnation with full restoration of constabulary status?

Promotion to a higher position within the Paris police? Yes, Prefect Javert, the highest constabulary rank in all of France. It once sounded so sweet. Now, in place of advancement, only harsh judgment and eternal condemnation await me.

Someone approaches.

"Who goes there? Identify yourself."

Chapter the Third:
An Undesired Companion

"Charles Francois Myriel, your fellow countryman in Earth time. In life, I had the honor of serving my Lord and Savior as priest, then Bishop of Digne, a small diocese nestled in the southeastern region of France."

"Digne, huh? A backwater town in a forgotten corner of our country. State your business… Most Reverend Bishop."

"I prefer that you address me simply as Charles."

"And you… Charles, shall address me as Inspector Javert."

"Ah, Javert, our coveted Earth titles hold little meaning here."

"I ask you, then, Charles, explain to me the nature of this 'here' you speak of?"

"For now, you may refer to this as Afterlife."

"After life? I know of no such place or condition. I command you, sir. Explain yourself clearly. Now!"

"You will find, my dear Javert, that your orders mean nothing in your new state of being."

"You speak in riddles, sir… Charles. I demand the truth, plain and simple."

"Upon your arrival, the Divine One in whom you believed and whom you professed to serve on Earth, assigned to me the honor of serving in the capacity of your personal greeter and guide."

"Greeter? Guide? Then I… I still live."

"Most assuredly. In your mother's womb you received the gift of unending life—"

"Do not speak of that woman! I rejected her the moment I came to understand she gave birth to me in a filthy prison cell, where she rightly spent the rest of her miserable life."

"It pains me to hear that. But on to the task at hand. Upon arrival here your life continues, albeit in a form as yet quite foreign to you."

"You call yourself a bishop."

"Yes."

"Of our Holy Roman Catholic Church."

"Indeed."

"Hah! Surely you mock me, Satan! I reject your disguise, you fake. In me, Javert—Inspector Javert to you—you have met your match. You do not fool me. I spent my entire career exposing liars and miscreants."

"I find your caution... reasonable, Javert. Nonetheless, in such position in life I did serve. Like me, you have left your earthly title and rank behind. Our mutual Father sees equality in all."

"Ah, now I see the truth! You too, Charles, bear the stain of an unrepentant sinner. We have arrived together at Hell's gate to await and soon share the fire that never consumes. I assure you, Son of Satan, I never sought a companion in life. Nor do I want to bare my soul to a fallen prelate of the Church.

"As my fellow policemen know well, I prefer to work alone because—and I state this with pride—none can match my sleuthing expertise. Partners pose an encumbrance. Officers of lower rank call me a lone wolf. And the most skilled police spy in all of France."

"So, you arrive here expecting a guilty verdict and a sentence of eternal fire?"

"What other fate might the likes of you and me deserve? A fallen guardian of the hallowed legal codes of France and a failed bishop of the Church. How grievously we paragons of moral righteousness betrayed our vocations!"

"Javert. I apologize for confusing you. Let me explain the purpose of my presence."

*　　　*　　　*

"I assure you, Javert, we do not stand at the rim of a fiery pit. Our one and most high God chose me to guide you through the required review of your life—in its entirety."

"Sir, you waste my time! Yours as well. I pride myself on unparalleled defense of law. I know an open-and-shut case when I see it. My instincts never failed me in… Earth life. They will not fail me in whatever you care to call this current state of existence. I know a man's crime and his fate long before the legal process grinds through the courts to a final verdict, which merely confirms my findings. So, Charles, shall we begin again? Explain to me your role here in what you refer to as… Afterlife?"

"Certainly. I have the pleasure, by divine assignment, of guiding you to your final destination."

"Guide me? A misleading euphemism. Guide me where? To the fires of Hell? I require no tour guide to lead the way on this my final excursion."

"The Creator and Savior of all sent me to receive you, Javert, and remain with you throughout this portion of your journey."

"How long will this take? As a man of action, I wait for no one. By the way, I seem to have misplaced my hat and coat which display the symbols of my rank and honors. I demand your leave to retrieve them."

"Oh, Javert, Javert. You shall soon learn that you left more than your uniform behind. You have discarded all such time-related accoutrements. In Afterlife we speak only in terms of the eternal Now."

"Do not play games with me! I know what I deserve, as well as my eternal destiny. I grow impatient with this meaningless preamble. Get on with my sentencing."

"You seem quite eager for your final judgment."

"Correct."

"To begin, Javert, may I ask your Christian name?"

"At my birth no one cared enough to endow me beyond my convict mother's surname. Through more than five decades of my life, I prided myself on having reversed the fate and reputation of my ignoble name and birth. My rank became my first name. I began as

Officer of the Law, then came my promotion to Chief of Police in Montreuil-Sur-Mer.

"And then, second in command of the prestigious Paris prefecture. In that capacity, I pledged to rid from our beloved capital's grand boulevards, streets, and byways every piece of underworld riffraff. And some day to ascend to the office of—Alas, Charles, that glorious day will never arrive, will it? I forfeited my career and glorious funeral parade along the Avenue des Champs-Élysées."

"Then, you have no need for further review."

"Exactly."

"And you find yourself guilty as charged and now pass judgment, sentencing yourself to eternal punishment where you expect to suffer unceasing hellfire."

"I do, Charles. I eagerly await serving out my sentence. I dislike word games—any games. When I demand a confession, I settle for nothing less than raw, unembellished truth. Cheats, liars, any wrongdoers falling into my net spend time in prison or the galleys, unless the feared guillotine claims priority. In truth, I consider death by the blade a merciful act."

"Javert, we have so much to discuss."

*   *   *

"Charles, let me clarify my response regarding my damning sin. In plain truth, I took my own life. There you have it. Clear and simple. Trial concluded. Sentencing set to begin right now!"

"Do you consider yourself a religious man?"

"I do. Considering the multiple demands on my time, I attend Mass when possible. I make a special effort on feast days relevant to France and her patron saints. I admire the way religion strengthens conscience. It keeps potential lawbreakers at bay—some of them at least. Your brothers in the cloth accept and obey the laws of the land and respect those who, like me, enforce our sacred statutes for the good order of society.

"Therefore, I believe in God as Father of all. But believe in God under the form of a crucified criminal Messiah? Never! A truly divine Son of God would show greater respect for the established laws of Moses and the Roman peacekeepers. Had I labored in police service in his day, that lawbreaker would have spent a far shorter time on planet Earth."

"I see, Javert. In truth, I don't but let's move on. What changed during the course of that fateful night on which you died?"

"To reference the Bible, Charles, as Jacob wrestled with his divine opponent, I wrestled with God through the whole of one night. I had sworn a solemn oath to obey and uphold the laws of the land to the day I died. In my last hour on earth, I… it shames me to admit this… I violated that Code for the first time since donning my uniform.

"What then? Return to headquarters—to my now sullied former life? Carry on as if nothing had changed? I deserved prison. Public disgrace. I shrunk like a coward from the prospect of facing exposure in the light of day. What a fall my mortal midnight crime!

"Can you imagine, Charles, what a disgraced officer of the law faces when sentenced to a life among prison inmates? Some of whom he arrested and sent to prison with a contented smile on his face and a sense of unreserved satisfaction. End my wretched life ripped apart by gleeful inmates? No thank you! 'What irony,' my former colleagues would say with a smirk as they gathered in their precinct headquarters. 'Inspector Javert died in a prison not unlike the one where his inmate-mother gave him birth. We should have known. Nothing good comes from uniting the soiled sperm of a criminal father and the ovum of a lowlife, gypsy mother.'

"In one night, I fell away from unquestioning adherence to law. And for this to occur on my last on earth? I betrayed the foundation upon which I had structured my entire life. My very existence. I exposed the folly of my life, laid it bare for public ridicule. How could I face the wretched horror of living even one more day on French soil? Having fallen from grace, I, the renowned and feared Inspector Javert, sought the coward's way out."

"Taking your own life."

"I stand here, Charles, before the throne of my divine Judge, prepared for endless damnation. I welcome my sentence. I hardly deserve to enter the Holy of Holies from whence he presides and rules over the hosts of heaven and the people of Earth, the faithful ones, at least."

*   *   *

"You seem quite certain about your eternal fate, Javert."

"You have before you a realist, Charles, not a philosopher. Nor one who pretends to possess knowledge and wisdom unknown to the rest of us levelheaded citizens. Self-aggrandizing thinkers only confuse the populace. They offer false hope that sinners can escape their rightly deserved punishment. May they all rot in Hell with me!"

"By your own word, you spent your life on the side of Michael's angels. What sort of punishment might you expect in light of your many years of service to God and country?"

"Did you not listen to me? My Creator and I know the nature of my sin. I deserve eternal—"

"Hellfire."

"Nothing less. No wink and a slap on the wrist for Inspector Javert. Now, sir, whatever your position or assignment, I owe you no further discourse. I prefer no audience, nor have I need of a companion to hold my hand. I shall pass through the Gates of Hell alone and head held high, thank you. In that manner I lived my life on Earth. And so will I descend into the fiery pit."

"My dear Javert, you have formed an erroneous assessment of my presence, my purpose. I assure you, you have arrived at a safe place. The One God, Creator of the universe, your God and mine, ordained that I should accompany and guide you through this final life review."

"Perhaps you misunderstand me, Charles. You see before you a man of action. Cause and effect. I repeat my confession of sin most grave and await the inevitable outcome.

"Only once in my life of honorable service did I violate my sworn duty as defender of our sacred Civil Code and right order in the society of mankind. I died unrepentant. I plead guilty to the charge and welcome my fate. Come, Divine Judge! Why the delay? Take me away. See what my failure, my one sin, cost me, Charles. Life. Liberty. Reward for a task superbly completed. Promotion to the high position I aimed for and deserved. I upheld the Law in its entirety, often risking my life… until my last shameful night."

"May I ask you, Javert, to share with me the final thing you remember from that scene?"

"You dare to ask me such a question? I, Javert, have no history of responding to any ad hoc inquisitor. If you had known me in life, heard of my stellar reputation, you would not dare to ask that question. I take pride in myself as the consummate professional, the best among my peers. I demand confessions, even if at times I resort to tactics I first learned as a police cadet and perfected beyond any of my peers. I carry out sentences proclaimed by judges, prison time or years at sea in the lightless filth of a galley ship. As I said, even death by the widow-making guillotine fails to match a lifetime in chains."

"Javert, it occurs to me that we have a mutual acquaintance."

*   *   *

"Charles, I will suffer no diversion from my fate. I prefer to get this… whatever you call it… over and done. I lived as a man of action. My profession demands quick and clear response. I pride myself on staying two steps ahead of the criminal class's devious machinations."

"I understand, Javert, but the man known to each of us still walks in Earth time. I met him only once. The two of you, I believe, had a lengthy history. What can you tell me about your relationship with a man named Jean Valjean?"

"You dare utter that name in my presence? I despise the very sound of it. When spoken, it sullies the air upon which it arrives in my ears. It's very intonation opens a floodgate that inundates me with distasteful memories. That man changed aliases as often as upper class females don new gowns… Madeleine… Fauchlevant… LeBlanc…. God alone knows what other pseudonyms and disguises. At the same time—"

"Why do you hesitate, Javert?"

"I cannot believe the words rushing to demand release. I despised the man but secretly… admired him. Never had such contradictory emotions battled for supremacy within me about one man, woman, or child."

"I confess, Javert, to struggling against similar clashes of feelings, though they arise from far different circumstances. May I share with you just a part of my own life story?"

"Must you?"

"I beg your indulgence."

"Make it short. My patience wears thin."

"Being of noble blood, albeit minor, when the revolution loomed, my father insisted that I flee France with my new bride—"

"A bride? You married as a priest? So, then, because of your infidelity we do enter hellfire together!"

"Allow me to explain. Shortly after I concluded all my university studies, my father arranged my marriage to a young woman. I had no say either in the decision to marry—or the choice of bride. Only after the passing of my dearest wife did I seek Holy Orders."

"I never heard such a thing."

"Allow me to make my point."

"If you must."

"Needless to say, I chafed at entering an arranged union with a woman I had yet to meet. Though most unhappy with the arrangement, I fell in love with her on our wedding night. Over the following weeks I grew to cherish my new bride and admitted—only to myself, of course—my father could not have found a better match. Nor could I have.

"When the first winds of revolution blew across Paris, he decided his son and daughter-in-law should seek safe refuge far from the revolution brewing at home. With reluctance and more than a little anxiety, my bride and I left our families and our beloved France to seek refuge in Italy."

"Dangerous times for those of you on the wrong side of history, Charles."

"Our journey by coach through the Alps, albeit in early summer, proved arduous. Making our way at times on foot proved taxing in the extreme for my bride. Our youth and growing love drove us to turn that hazardous relocation into a shared adventure.

"We embraced the prospect of life in a strange new land, free from parental and societal scrutiny. Italy, we discovered, offered more than a safe haven from France's upheaval. As we made our way south from Lago di Como, we entered a magical paradise of lush, fragrant orchards and endless vineyards. And floral abundance beyond anything we had witnessed at home.

"While we missed our families desperately, I admit we enjoyed immediate and compassionate acceptance among our new olive-completcted neighbors. We relished their warm, life-embracing approach to life.

"We settled in the historic and magical city of emperors and popes. Learning a new language excited us and gave us freedom to explore Rome's endless adventures, its myriad historical sites and precious treasures. Each day we sought out monuments chronicling the empire's origins and myths. At the heart of Rome, of course, lay Vatican City and St. Peter's Basilica, home to the Holy See and its own magnificent history, its Renaissance art and unsurpassed architecture.

"All the while, we worried about the fate of our families at home, the perils they might face as we roamed freely at our leisure. We found a small villa in a settlement offering all we needed. One Sunday, not long after our arrival, we discovered the Church of Santa Francesca Romana. Forgive me, Javert. Surely, you have little interest in my youthful escapades."

"About that, Charles, you stand correct. I mean no insult, but every word you speak delays my judgment and entrance into Hell's hungry fires."

*　　　*　　　*

"I agree it seems foreign at first. Trust me, you will adjust. In Afterlife, Javert, Earth time becomes meaningless. The same for past and future. You have entered what we call here the Eternal Now.

You will know no other dimension. Nonetheless, I shall abbreviate my story to focus on your life journey.

"My spouse and I dreamed of raising a large family. Our lovemaking took us to the heights of ecstasy, but the good Lord designed another plan for us. We did not conceive. Near the end of our first year in Rome, she contracted a lung infection that, sadly, claimed her life, but only after causing gut-wrenching suffering—and for me a broken heart. When she passed, I fell into the throes of abandonment and despair. We had yet to reach our second anniversary.

"Less than a year later—the worst period of my life—I felt a call to revive my long-neglected faith. And later of all things—and to my utmost shock and surprise—God reached deep into my soul and called me to priesthood. No one could have predicted such an outcome. Not I. Not my family in France.

"In letter after letter, my father did all he could to dissuade me. He called my desire to serve our Lord Jesus as a priest an 'abomination on the Myriel family name.' After my ordination, I remained in Italy until it became safe to return again to France."

"How sweet, Charles, but get to the point. I would hear more about this man whose path crossed both our lives."

*   *   *

"Sometime after my appointment to serve as bishop of Digne, I encountered a famished and bedraggled parolee. He introduced himself as Jean Valjean—"

"The man I despise most in all the world! Go on."

"I met him only the once. He pounded on our door while we sat at our evening meal. We invited him to share our supper, which he devoured in less than a minute. I convinced him to pass the night in a warm, clean bed in our home. To shorten the story—"

"Please do."

"Valjean left us the following day after I convinced a trio of gendarmes I freely bestowed on him our purloined family silver.

I never saw or heard of him again. My only point, Javert? Just that Valjean stands between us as a common link."

"Tell me, Charles, does he still live?"

"He does. I know nothing more about the man."

CHAPTER THE FOURTH:
A CHILD IN PRISON

"If I may ask, Charles, how long must I wait for this… this process to conclude? Javert never waits in line—for anything."

"All newcomers to Afterlife soon grow accustomed to leaving time behind them, as well as place, profession, national origin. In your present state, these dimensions have little meaning. But I do understand your resistance. We all face the same shock the instant our soul separates from its lifelong Earth companion."

"Hmpf!"

"Have no fear, my son. My commission calls me to guide you safely through what may appear an endless maze."

"Safely? You mean ensconced forever within Hell's eternal torment."

"Javert, I serve only as your guide through this life review. Then comes your final judgment over which I have no control."

"Fine. I confess that, after dedicating my entire life to strict interpretation of our ordinances, I committed an unpardonable sin. The end!"

"Unpardonable?"

"Indeed. I set a guilty man free, thereby violating a sacred statute of French Law. That same law demands a sentence worse than death—eternal damnation. I accept my fate and ask nothing more."

"You have much yet to learn, Javert. Let us begin with the understanding that neither you nor I have charge of this process. I expect you to find this uncomfortable, tedious even. In truth, you have no option other than to accept it as a fact of your new existence."

"You have spoken rightly, Charles. I do object. I intend no insult, but I appeal to a higher authority. I demand an audience before your immediate superior."

"Javert, you speak the truth. I do not stand on the top rung of heaven's ladder. Far from it, but I assure you, no matter your discomfort, I must fulfill my appointed duty to guide you through a full examen of your Earth life. Upon conclusion of this journey, our Divine and Just Judge will decree your eternal fate."

*   *   *

"Return to the time and place of your birth, Javert."

"Must I?"

"Yes. You will find it impossible to hold back anything of relevance."

"How do you expect me to—"

"Every instant of your life engraved an indelible imprint on your soul."

"I… I do see it… yes! The year 1780. Horror of horrors. A dank and filthy cell in the women's prison somewhere out on the west coast of France. …I see a woman in distress. She shrieks in pain and terror. …While still in the womb I hear the woman curse the father of her unwanted child, spewing a litany of foul vitriol against him… also at the uncaring God she never believed in. She damns this new creature struggling to quit her womb. She wishes it, begs this new being, male or female, to drop from her womb devoid of life. …Upon my arrival in the world, I sense her sister inmates assisting at my birth. …I recall as a young boy wishing I had obliged her and fallen into the world having already left it behind."

"A sad tale indeed. Tell me about your mother."

"I hated her from my first gasping wail. A curse on that damned Bohemian! A gipsy. Lowest scum of the earth. A criminal rightly removed from respectable society. I learned as a child that she earned her way as a fortuneteller, until she ran afoul of the law for picking her clients' pockets while predicting lives of fame and fortune. She found herself pregnant without a responsible husband to provide for her and their bastard child.

"I sent legions like her to prison over the course of my career. In each female lawbreaker, I saw her image. Every arrest infused me with intense satisfaction that I had punished my mother for living a dissolute life. Primarily, I hated her for allowing me to enter her disgusting world alive."

"And your father? What do you know of him?"

"Another lowlife scoundrel. I don't know his name—never wanted to. I wanted nothing to do with either of them. I later learned that, at the time of my birth, he suffered the hard labor pains of half-life on the galleys. I never encountered him face to face, for which I consider myself most fortunate. For him too, as I would have haunted him to the day he died."

"He died a prisoner?"

"So the story goes, Charles, but I have no proof. Never cared to inquire. My hope at this moment? That Hell's breadth and depth will prevent us from ever meeting face to face. All my life I regretted my name, bestowed by the woman from whose womb I entered this world. She hadn't the generosity even to bestow upon me a saint's name. From the beginning and forever, I remained simply Javert. My mother's surname or one she conjured from thin air. As I grew to manhood, I took for myself as a first name, each rank as I ascended the sacred ladder of law enforcement. Thus, I arrive before my Just Judge head held high as *Inspector* Javert, second in command of the Paris Prefecture, commissioned police spy of—nearly—spotless record in the service of the Republic of France."

"How sad, my son."

"Your pity mocks me, sir!"

"Let me repeat—despite your certitude—the outcome of this review remains shrouded in mystery. Upon arrival here in Afterlife, we discover we have—and always had—a personal birth name by which God alone knows us. Some few discover their God-name during their lifetime. The vast majority of humans do not."

*   *   *

"Let us continue. Tell me about your childhood years, Javert."

"By the age of four, I had come to see that life offered me but two choices. Adopt the Bohemian, criminal ways of my parents—the detritus of human society—who sowed the bad seed that became my life."

"Or?"

"Choose the only other path the circumstances of my ignoble birth offered."

"Law enforcement."

"Yes, to spend my life in the service of right order. I vowed, in my child's way, to uphold the righteous classes of society—royalty, businessmen, politicians, scholars, officers of the law, and yes, the clergy. These I kept safe from the likes of those two craven souls, who chose the dark lifepath of dishonor. The broad highway to Hell."

"And Jean Valjean?"

"I command you not to utter that name in my presence!"

"You find it so detestable?"

"Had he not tempted me, I would still live in honor, using the finely honed skills of my calling to ensnare his kind and usher them to live out their days in the manner such criminals deserve."

"Tell me more about how you escaped the fate you so abhorred as a child?"

"I ingratiated myself to the prison guards. They let me run errands, carry messages. They trusted me to deliver them with accuracy and haste. Whatever task they gave me I fulfilled, never making a careless mistake... not one. In the Commandant and the officers under his command, I discovered my true family, Charles. My rightful sires. They took note of my diligence. The Commandant became my mentor, taking me under his personal tutelage. I desired to model myself after him in every way. Over time, I grew into a dedicated, single-minded, and lifelong servant of my country.

"The Commandant demanded tight discipline among his officers, showed no pity to inmates. By my every word and gesture, I displayed my desire to escape, not only that prison but the ugly scar of my ignoble birth, my clear-pathed destiny to life as a criminal. I bent the iron bars of my personal cell, my identity as son of the damned, and cast my lot with the police. In time, I caught the attention of a new Commandant. As I grew into budding manhood, my path in life came into sharper focus."

"Clearly, you found happiness as you advanced in age."

"Bah! I never yearned for that grand illusion you like to call 'happiness.' Ask me about satisfaction, advancement in rank. Yes. In these I found a measure of peace. If that defines what you call 'happiness,' I answer with a wholehearted affirmation. I never doubted the wisdom of my life path, not as long as a single lawbreaker remained at large on the streets of France. Nor did I question the rectitude of my calling until... until those final hours of my life."

*   *   *

"You never married, then, Javert."

"Have you understood nothing, sir? I considered a wife a rival to the demands of my profession, which required my full attention and commitment—day and night, every day of the week. I remained faithful to my chosen 'spouse'... until I committed the single, damning sin of professional adultery.'"

"Never a woman in your life, then."

"Must you search for scabs and pick at them? Alright. Once, in my youth, a young woman sought to turn my head. One evening over supper in her father's cafe, she put her cards on the table, so to speak. 'I love you, Javert.' She loved me! No one had ever spoken those words in my presence. I pretended not to hear and continued eating. Then I left, never to return."

"Tell me about her, if you would."

"Though momentarily distracted, I had nothing within me to share with any other mortal, let alone a marital partner. My profession took precedence over the companionship of any woman, whether spouse, mother, sister, or friend. Having closed and padlocked that iron-barred gate, I never looked back."

"Thank you for your directness."

"And you? Not a little mistress on the side? I've seen too much in my career to trust any vowed celibate."

"Since I asked you the question, I cannot shirk an honest answer."

"Hah! I thought so. That explains why we meet at the gates of Hell."

"I have shared with you my story of love and romance. As you know, it did not last long—"

"So, Charles, tell me your sad tale of life as clandestine adulterer in priest's clothing."

"I regret having to disappoint you, Javert, but you have it all wrong. Recall that I told you earlier I did not leave my wife. She left me. After that, I had no desire for the affection of any other woman. As I advanced in my ministry, work demanded all of me, both body and soul."

"See, Charles, we share the same passion, you and I, in our dedication to our vocations. Why delay further? I have no use for frivolous conversation?"

"Very well. Let's move on."

CHAPTER THE FIFTH:
A CULPABLE ACT GOES UNPUNISHED

"Where do we find ourselves now, Charles?"

"You should recognize your former jurisdiction, the town of Montreuil-sur-Mer. You held the office of Chief of Police.

"In the Region of Calais in northwest France. I know the place well."

"Tell me about your time there."

"I curse its name and all the people in it. That includes its former Mayor, Monsieur Madeleine—known to you as Jean Valjean."

"What happened in this town that you wish to review?"

"What I wish? You know my only desire. To terminate this 'review,' as you insist on calling it, and enter the flames of eternal hellfire."

"Then begin, Javert. You authored your life story and now play the role of protagonist."

*   *   *

"Word spread quickly among the citizens. Their new Chief of Police allowed no crime to go unpunished. No matter the perpetrator's pleas of innocence. I accepted only the truth. In its entirety. My unflinching attitude and demeanor allowed the citizens of Montreuil-sur-Mer only two valid civic sentiments, respect for authority and aversion to crime of any sort.

"I defined for the town the following forms of malfeasance: murder, robbery, prostitution, public disturbance plus any and all crimes, no matter how minor, no exceptions. I reject the euphemism, misdemeanor. Therefore, I scorned in disgust any man, woman, or child above the age of reason who crossed the threshold of evil. I brooked no mournful pleas of 'extenuating circumstances' or talk of how much time had intervened since original crime and the culprit's capture. At the other end of the human scale stood the goodhearted, law-abiding citizens."

"And they consisted of…?"

"I already told you. Anyone who held an official function. From the mayor to the lowest rank of the police force. No one lawfully serving in a public office, whether high or low, could ever do wrong. But—Something about our much-loved mayor, Monsieur Madeleine, seemed to me… awry. The townsfolk loved—dare I say—venerated him as a living saint. Still… a strange, undefinable itch afflicted my long-term memory. This despite the businessman's peerless reputation as a wealthy, upright man, renowned throughout the region for his generosity toward those of lower station… those I prefer to call the 'criminal class.'

"'I know this man from somewhere,' I thought. No. …Yes. Conflicting memories competed within my brain. An image from the past. The quarry at Toulon prison. Over a decade had passed since our strongest, most tireless convict earned his parole, after nineteen years in our prison system. My vehement recommendation to extend the man's sentence failed to prevail.

"I challenged my memory to produce a connection, an identity. One day I remembered Prisoner 24601's full name… Jean Valjean. Could it be? Of course! The charade I uncovered but never shared convinced me. The scumbag Mayor's current name and position disguised a clever and most devious lie."

"How did you proceed with your… certainty?"

"At first, I dared not identify our Mayor as the same man. What former convict ever ascended from the lowest level of humanity's filthy and illiterate scum to become a successful, well-endowed inventor and employer of so many, let alone a revered mayor? No paroled convict in memory had achieved the wealth and universal acclaim and respect of all who knew him. Comparing this beloved man to the incorrigible thief of my past dangled in the outermost realm of possibility. I, the peerless Inspector Javert, remained the only citizen of the region to reserve judgment on our... sainted mayor's status in decent society."

"Proceed, Javert. I love a mystery, whether divine or quite human."

CHAPTER THE SIXTH:
JAVERT PUT IN HIS PLACE

"**L**ate one frigid night, a disturbance erupted in an unsavory district within our township. That particular area grew more dangerous in the post-sunset hours. Honest citizens put their own selves at risk entering that thief and diseased prostitute-infested zone. From the shouting I heard upon my approach, I surmised a pickpocket or one of the area's filthy whores had accosted one of our honorable man who mistakenly ventured into that neighborhood. Wielding my cudgel, I thrust aside the shouting spectators and gained entrance to the roiling inner circle."

"'Chief Javert, this foul witch attacked me as I passed along minding my own business,' attested Monsieur Bamatabnois, the victim. Himself a businessman of our town.

"I took hold of the bedraggled prostitute, the lowest form of femininity. Often, women of her ilk put up a fight upon arrest. Not this one. Nearly bald and missing most of her teeth, she yielded to my grasp like a worn-out doll that had lost its stuffing. I demanded her name.

"She brushed away a tear and whimpered, 'Fantine.' Never had I heard a more raspy, guttural voice.

"The odor of filth and God knows what else emanated from the culprit's body. She disgusted me. Clearly, I'd need to change uniforms once back at the stationhouse. 'Surname?'

"I—I don't know, sir… or no longer remember."

"Clearly, this slut knew the routine, therefore must have faced arrest in the past. She could expect to spend this night in jail awaiting conviction and sentencing for accosting a man of substance.

"With her firmly in my grasp, I set out with long strides, dragging her along the cobbled lanes. Our station sat at one corner of the main square. On the way, I uttered not a word. Nor did she. A crowd of spectators followed in a party mood, jeering at my captive and shouting foul curses I shall not repeat in your august company, Charles.

"On arrival at the station, I opened the door, entered with my catch, and slammed the door behind me. 'Let no one enter,' I commanded the sentry, to the great disappointment of the howling crowd. Instead, their faces filled the station's windows. Children and shorter adults raised themselves on the tips of their toes, craning their necks in an effort to peer inside. Curiosity becomes a form of gluttony, does it not, Charles? The spewing of hatred debases the soul. The harlot fell into a corner like a pile of overturned dirt. She crouched like a terrified cur. Motionless. Mute.

"French law consigned this sort of woman entirely to the discretion of the local police. We did as we saw fit to prevent them from further accosting society's virtuous citizens. Severe punishment more than fit the gravity of this one's crime, along with confiscation of any ill-gotten wages of her sinful existence.

"For my part, I assumed my usual impassive demeanor. The sergeant of the guard brought a lighted candle to my writing table. I took a seat and withdrew a quarter-fold sheet of paper from my inside breast pocket. Without delay, I set to writing an incident report in my accustomed meticulous detail. I had learned over the years that my silence had a more terrifying effect on those in custody than an outpouring of threatening words.

"As I stated, laws governing this case gave me discretion to act as her accuser, judge, and jury… and yes, jailer as well. In my notes I wrote what I saw. The accused had willfully attacked a highly respected pillar of our community.

"The more I reviewed this woman's deeds, the more my disgust for her grew. She not only insulted but attacked the poor fellow. Decent society cannot tolerate the sort of criminality I interrupted. I wrote in silence, 'A prostitute identifying herself by the single name,

Fantine, attacked a prominent citizen with intent to inflict life-threatening harm.'

"When finished, I signed the paper, folded it, and addressed the sergeant of the guard, 'Take three men and confine this creature to a cell.' I turned to Fantine, 'You will serve six months' incarceration.'

"The woman paled and shuddered. 'Prison! Six months in which to earn a meager seven sous a day! What will become of Cosette? My daughter! My poor, helpless child. I owe those Thenardiers over a hundred francs. Surely, you understand my plight, Monsieur Inspector.'

"Horror flamed in her eyes as she dragged herself across the dusty floor. 'Inspector Javert, I beseech your mercy. If you had witnessed my innocence from the beginning, you would treat me with respect. I swear to you by the good God above, I had no blame in this matter! That... gentleman, whom I do not know, took my body for his pleasure, then poured snow down my back. Has anyone the right to put snow down a woman's back when she does no harm? I suffer an illness, as you can see. That man spat on me and shouted, 'Look at yourself, you toothless hag! Cropped head. Filthy clothing. Your ugliness stains this Godfearing township.'

"'I know only too well I no longer have my teeth... or my hair. I sold them to raise a little money to pay for my child's upkeep with the Thenardier family. I assure you, I dealt with this man in a most respectful manner. Ask the people around us who witnessed it. I confess I did wrong to make him angry. I reacted instinctively... lost control but only in that first moment of shock. I regret having spoiled that gentleman's hat. Where did he go? Bring him here. I will humbly beg his pardon. I will. You'll see.'

"She ranted on, 'Oh, my God! I see now it makes no difference if I beg his pardon. Chief Javert, I beg you, grant me clemency today—just this one time. If I don't pay one hundred francs, those innkeepers will toss my little girl into the frozen midwinter streets where she'll surely die. Oh, my Cosette! In this weather! My little angel of the Holy Virgin. I cannot have her with me. What I do each night to pay her upkeep disgusts me. What might it do to my innocent child to see me in this state? The Thenardiers insist on having their money. They want it tomorrow. Tomorrow! I beg you, sir, have pity on me.'

"What a sad, tragic story, Javert."

"Sad indeed, Charles, that such women should besmirch our society."

"Still your heart remained unmoved?"

"Not a millimeter. I've dealt with countless whores. Each with a sad tale excusing her vile trade."

"Her pleas meant nothing, Javert? You knew she spoke the truth."

"The truth? Truth lies in my service to the law. Whatever her motives, they made no difference. Surely you know that the Law punishes deeds, not motives. I cannot count the number of times I nabbed a woman like her. I've heard and ignored the heartrending wails of countless bare-breasted slime, confessing their sorrow and wringing their hands. I've seen it all, I assure you. Overseeing the galley ships and laborers at Toulon had hardened my resolve to allow no exceptions—ever. Most criminals, like this one, come into my grasp choked by dry coughs, struggling to speak of their blameless agony and despair.

"To this one, I snarled, 'I have heard you out, woman. Six months in the women's prison ought to deter you from ever again repeating your crime. Now march!' Charles, our Eternal Father in person would do the same."

"I shall not try to convince you otherwise. Tell me more about this benighted woman. Fantine, I believe you called her?"

"Yes. I grant she put on quite a show for the policemen present and the jeering mob outside. She wrung her intertwined fingers and wailed for mercy! Mercy, can you believe it?"

"What became of her?"

"During her futile tirade, a man appeared to have slipped past the distracted sentry unnoticed.'"

* * *

"In the commotion of the moment, no one paid any heed to this newcomer. At the very instant my officers grabbed hold of the woman to raise her to her feet, the intruder emerged from the shadows. I raised my eyes and recognized—can you believe?—our Mayor, Monsieur Madeleine.

"'One moment, if you please.' He spoke calmly but with steel in his voice. 'Release this woman.'

"In my sternest but reserved tone, I acknowledged his presence. 'Monsieur Mayor—' This interruption of police business produced a curious effect upon our prisoner. She rose to her feet and, in a single bound, thrust aside my officers' grip and flung herself at Madeleine.

"Before anyone could corral her, she screamed, 'It's you, Monsieur Mayor!' She burst into a terrifying fit of hate-filled laughter—and spit in his face!"

$$* \qquad * \qquad *$$

"I tell you, Charles, to see a woman of the streets spit in the face of an honorable official and strike him repeatedly—I struggled to comprehend the grievance at the root of such a vile and relentless attack. An assault so monstrous I regarded it a sacrilege. Even in the confusion of the moment, I wondered what kind of man our Mayor could be. What punishment had he inflicted on this woman to merit such a violent response? Had he too used her body and walked away refusing to toss her even a centime?

"Amid all this, I had not registered the fact that our Mayor had overridden my authority. Had he truly ordered me to release her? Set this homicidal prostitute at liberty? I suffered a paralysis of amazement. All thought failed me. Not finding words, I remained mute.

"As for that Fantine woman, the Mayor's words triggered a strange effect. Suddenly alert and sober, she turned to face me.

"'I must have heard those words of liberty from your mouth, honorable Chief Javert.'

"Never had I witnessed such a reversal of emotion. A moment ago, a mad woman, a whirling dervish. An instant later, calm reigned. A hopeful smile creased her ugly face.

"'May I go free then? Not to prison?' She pointed a crooked, bony finger at the Mayor. 'Yes, make sport at my expense. Did you hear the Chief of Police decree that I have regained my freedom? You will let me go then, sir. That monster of a Mayor, that old blackguard, caused my troubles. Imagine, Monsieur Javert. Based on false rumors he took my employment away, cast me into the street! Why? He believed the gossip of a pack of rascally coworkers, women telling lies in the workroom. If that counts not as a horror, tell me what does. To dismiss a poor girl doing her work honestly! That horrible man left me with no honorable way to earn a living and pay for my sweet Cosette's upkeep.'

"She gestured to her ripped and soiled garments. 'All this... misery... followed. I will explain it to you, Inspector,' she went on. 'I had no choice but to earn my way however I could. I grew up as a decent, Godfearing child and young woman... except for one weekend with a well-to-do young man. I fell in love. He promised we would marry if I would.... Since then, I have lived for my daughter, God's gift to me in the wake of my sin.'

"Again she pointed an unsteady finger at the Mayor. 'All that ended the day that blackguard of a Mayor tossed me to the wolves, forcing me into the fallen woman life you behold today. So, now you understand. I did not sin deliberately. In your great wisdom, Honorable Chief, you not only understood but also commanded your officers to set me free... did you not?'

"Monsieur Madeleine listened with profound attention, while she spoke. He fumbled in his waistcoat, drew out his purse and opened it. Empty, it seemed. Putting it back in his pocket, he addressed Fantine, 'How much did you say you owed your daughter's caregivers?'

"Fantine turned in a rage to face the Mayor again. 'You wretch of a Mayor, you came here to frighten me. You can see how sickness has taken hold of me. Day and night I suffer an unceasing cough. A doctor demanded three sous before giving this empty advice, 'Take care of yourself.'

"She no longer wept but smiled. She adjusted her disordered garments, dropping the folds of her dress which had crept to her knees. She stepped toward the door but turned to address my officers. In a firm voice, each word carefully pronounced, she instructed them, 'Did you not hear your superior officer?' She put one hand on the latch but stopped. One step more and she would reach the street. '*Monsieur l'Inspecteur* ordered you to release me. Now I go.'

"The sound of the latch roused me from my stupor. I raised my head and barked with authority, 'Sergeant! Don't you see her walking off! Which of you promised her freedom?'

"'I gave her leave to go!'

"The Mayor! Fantine turned as if invisible claws had clutched her. Without uttering a word, her glance strayed from Mayor Madeleine to me and, in turn, from me to the Mayor.

"A violent quiver wracked my body. 'That cannot be.'

"'Why not, Javert?' asked the Mayor.

"'This wretched woman insulted an honorable citizen on the street. Now, in your august presence she dared to defy my authority. Emboldened by your intervention, let me add.'

"'Inspector Javert,' our Mayor replied in his calm—but to me infuriating—manner. 'Listen closely to what I say.'"

"And did you, Javert? Truly listen?"

"I did, Charles, wondering what insult he might inflict in the presence of my subordinates, an offense for which I would soon repay him with all the authority of my office.

"'Chief Javert, in you I see an honorable man and faithful servant of our common homeland. Therefore, I shall explain the situation calmly, man to man. I begin with the true state of this case: I passed through the square at the moment you led this woman away. Unlike you, I made inquiries among witnesses to the entire scene from beginning to end. I learned a great deal about the alleged scuffle. That upstanding townsman, Monsieur Bamatabnois, charge him as the true criminal in this case. He deserves arrest, not this desperate woman.'"

"'See here! You cannot override my decision. This wretch of a woman just insulted you, Monsieur, in my presence. That alone counts as a punishable offense. Since she has no money to pay a fine, the law requires that she serve time in the women's prison workhouse until she earns enough to pay her fine—'

"The mayor interrupted me. 'Now, listen well to what concerns me, Inspector. I merited this poor woman's insult. I take responsibility for her fall from grace. Now I shall do what I must to make amends.'

"'I strongly differ with the Mayor's conclusion.'

"Monsieur Madeleine then hurled an affront of his own. 'There exists a higher law than your manmade statutes.'

"'A... a higher law? Nonsense!' I withheld a snort.

"He came back with, 'You will not find true justice in the laws found in your manmade statutes, Javert. The Master Lawgiver, our Father in heaven, reserves to himself the final judgment of right and wrong. I have heard this woman. She speaks the truth.'

"'We seem at an impasse, Monsieur. A higher law? Bah! You see what you imagine.'

"Charles, listen to this. Madeleine had the audacity to add, right in front of the woman and my fellow officers, 'Content yourself, then, with obeying your own laws. In accordance with those same statutes, within a defined jurisdiction, the Chief of Police serves at the pleasure of a township's Mayor. My office makes me your superior. You, therefore, serve the people of Montreuil-sur-Mer, not on your own authority. Or did you forget?'

"'On the contrary, sir, I demand this woman shall serve six months in prison.'"

"'I have spoken, Inspector Javert! Heed this well. Fantine will not spend one single night in your jail. I declare this on the authority of my mayoral office. There! You have my final word on the matter.'"

"And how did you respond to that, Javert?"

"At this decisive word, I too lowered my voice but did not surrender a gram of my authority. 'With due respect, I oppose your decision.'

"Never in my life had I permitted anyone to override my lawful decree. In my defense I argued, 'By your own admission, I, not you, witnessed the crime scene. Let me review for your benefit the indisputable facts of this case. This... woman flung herself on the victim, Monsieur Bamatabnois, the owner of a handsome residence cut entirely of stone. It stands three stories high. Its balcony overlooks a lovely esplanade.'

"I explained all this, Charles, as if instructing a new recruit. 'In any case, Monsieur Mayor, her crime falls within my legal jurisdiction as Chief of Police. I used my righteous authority to pass judgment. Whether it suits you or not, I shall detain this woman.'

"I dared not show weakness in front of my underlings. What sort of example would that present to them about conducting by-the-book police business?

"Instead of backing down, Monsieur Madeleine folded his arms. He spoke in a severe voice which no one in the town had hitherto heard, 'Let... me... repeat, Javert. The matter to which you refer falls under Articles nine, eleven, fifteen, and sixty-six of the applicable Criminal Code. These articles clearly give the Mayor authority and discretion to override actions of the Chief of Police. Let me also refer you to Article eighty-one of a law passed on December 13, 1799, regarding arbitrary detention. Based on the statutes just quoted, I declare as your superior that you must set this woman at liberty. If you value at all your position here in Montreuil-sur-Mer, you will not stand in opposition to my removal of this poor sick woman from your custody. In short, Inspector, I forbid you to speak another word on this matter.'

"Taking this blow full in the face, I forced an exaggerated bow before the mayor, turned my back, and exited the room."

"Javert, I feel the pain you suffered in sharing your confrontation with your superior. So that ended the affair?"

"I conceded that Madeleine had won the first round. Ever after, I nursed a wound that never healed. I vowed to await my opportunity to repay him tenfold for my humiliation and the damage to my authority."

"And did you, Javert, have your day of triumph?"

"Not right away, Charles. But I kept alive a never-fading image of Jean Valjean. With that, let me now share, with great reluctance, my next direct encounter with the Mayor."

CHAPTER THE SEVENTH:
AN APOLOGY

"Charles, six weeks after the events I just described, I strode from my office to the Mayor's. I had distressing news to share. Unaccustomed to admitting fault, I yielded to a compelling truth. More than once on my way, I stopped, turned on my heels and took a step in the direction of the precinct. Only to right myself, turn, and keep walking.

I summoned all my strength, inhaled a deep breath, and approached his door. Entering the room in silence, I stood erect, bicorn hat in hand, my eyes cast down in respect before the seated Mayor. He did not look up. Nor did I wish to interrupt the business that appeared to demand his full attention. I waited and remained so until it pleased him to acknowledge me.

"Without looking up from the documents on his desk, he addressed me curtly but without rancor. 'Yes, Javert?'

"I responded solemnly and with force. 'Monsieur Mayor, duty binds me to report that someone within your jurisdiction has committed a culpable act.'

"Mayor Madeleine looked up but remained silent for a moment before he spoke. 'Chief Javert, describe for me this person's crime.'

"'I must report that a lesser agent of the authorities failed in the gravest manner towards a magistrate. Therefore, as Chief of Police, I must bring this crime to your attention.'

"His eyes revealed surprise but not the least curiosity. I considered that... odd. 'How does this misconduct concern me? Certainly, you have full authority to deal with the situation, whatever the crime and its perpetrator.'

"'In this case, Monsieur Mayor, only you can take action.'

"'Then, tell me the name of that agent?'

"On the way to his office, I had prepared to serve as my own accuser, jury, and judge. Without engaging his eyes, I confessed, 'The one who stands before you.'

"'You, Javert?'

"'Yes.'

"Madeleine registered—how might I describe his perplexing demeanor? Surprise? Far too weak a tag to encompass his expression. Alarm? Closer, yet his features remained passive.

"'May I ask the name of the offended magistrate?'

"I mustered all my professional strength. 'You, sir.' The Mayor sat motionless. His pen hand froze in midair. Eyes cast down, I added, 'I have come to request that you relieve me of my duties as Chief of Police. I shall hand in my resignation here and now.'

"With that, I stopped, expecting him to respond. His silence chilled my bones. What graver, more severe punishment might he contemplate? I had more to say. 'Sir, you treated me badly by overriding my judgment with regard to that prostitute.'

"'That destitute young mother has a name, Javert. Fantine. At this moment, she lies gravely ill in our hospital, ministered to by our good Sisters of Charity.'

"I took a deep breath to steady my nerves. 'Nonetheless, I dare say you damaged my authority in the presence of my junior officers, for whom I set a high bar of professional conduct and demand compliance in every respect. Today, I come before you, expecting you to impose the proper punishment for my crime.'

"The Mayor seemed not to comprehend the context of my maltreatment. Could he so quickly have forgotten his behavior that night and my reactions? I filled the gap. 'Over a month ago. In my police headquarters. The scene you stirred over that woman you yourself had the prior good judgment to dismiss from your employ.'

"'I repeat, Javert, the one you refer to as *that woman* has a proper name.'

"'Sir, may I remind you that… Fantine… a woman of ill repute, spat in the face of an honorable gentleman, yourself, right in my station before a dozen or more witnesses. They will verify that criminal behavior. She deserved extended jail time. Six months, perhaps longer.'

"'I assure you, Inspector, I did not intend to cause you embarrassment. I offer no apology, but I do see how I might have offended you. If you have nothing further to say, I thank you for your candor. Let me assure you I have neither the intention nor the desire to take this matter further.'

"Charles, I had little interest in sparring with him over my choice of words. Releasing a sigh from the bottom of my chest, I addressed the Mayor. 'I have something more to add. It has nothing to do with… Fantine.'

*   *   *

"Madeleine fixed me with his gaze. I wondered why he persisted in concealing his true state of mind. His dark eyes revealed that my words had at least opened him to acknowledge the possible consequences for his Chief of Police. But not for himself until I raised the stakes. 'Monsieur Mayor, I informed against you, at whose pleasure I serve.' Madeleine's body stiffened. 'As this town's most superior officer I performed my sworn duty. I reported you as the escaped convict, Jean Valjean.'

"'I see.' Madeleine's voice revealed neither admission nor rejection. 'And to whom did you submit this accusation?'

"I took another deep breath, Charles, and continued the confession which would sully my hitherto impeccable career. 'I reported you to the Prefect of Paris Police.'

"'May I ask why?'

"'A resemblance given flesh months ago when I witnessed your rescue of old man Fauchelevant from under his collapsed wagon.'

"The Mayor remained calm. Dare I say, disinterested? 'Tell me more about this… convict you speak of.'"

"On leaving prison, he robbed a holy Bishop in the southern diocese of Digne. Shortly after that, he flaunted the laws of society by committing another cowardly theft against the person of a young Savoyard on a public roadway.'"

"Javert, let me remind you that the parolee you speak of did not steal our family's heirloom silver plates and candlesticks. I freely surrendered them. Beyond that fact, I know nothing more about his life or what became of him. Not until now."

"I swear to you, Charles, in my professional judgment, once a felon always a criminal at heart. Valjean dropped from sight a number of years ago. Forgotten by everyone, it seemed… but me. Yes, for a time his face haunted the walls of precincts over the length and breadth of France. But forget all that for the moment. I confessed to denouncing my legal superior."

"I can imagine your quandary, Javert. How did Monsieur Madeleine respond to your revelation?"

"He neither moved nor spoke… until he asked with an air of patient indifference, 'And did you receive a reply from Paris?'

"'I did. The Prefect himself sent word to me by post. It arrived at the station yesterday in the late afternoon.'

"'And?'

"'It seems I had it wrong. Though I see a resemblance in you, the police near Arras have arrested the real Jean Valjean. He now occupies a cell in that city. The circuit court currently meets there to try regional cases. His trial begins tomorrow morning. Since I have firsthand experience with this Valjean fellow, the judge summoned me to testify.'

"At those words, Charles, the sheet of paper the Mayor held slipped from his hand to the cluttered desktop. He raised his head and fixed me in his gaze, as if acknowledging my presence for the first time. He breathed a drawn out 'Ahhh!' I took that as a dismissal, but I had not yet concluded my report.

"'The word I received, Monsieur Mayor, revealed there dwelt in a neighborhood around Ailly-le-Haut-Clocher a fellow living under the alias, Champmathieu. A wretched creature. A lifelong thief. The police charged him with a heinous act. I blame him not for eschewing his true name, John Valjean.'

"I paused, expecting the Mayor to ask the nature of the crime.

When he showed not the slightest interest, I continued. 'He scaled an orchard wall to steal cider apples, breaking some tree branches in the process. When arrested, he still held one of the fruit-laden branches in his hand. They immediately locked the scamp in a cell to await trial.'

"The mayor's face tightened with annoyance. 'None of this happened within our jurisdiction, Javert. Why bring it to me?'

"Charles, allow me tell you what occurred next. Divine Providence favored the side of the law. It happened that a few hardened prisoners who had spent time with Valjean in Toulon prison happened, by God's providence, to have shared the same lock-up as the accused. One named, I believe it was Brevet, recognized him. He identified the apple thief as none other than our long-pursued Jean Valjean! With this, I had Monsieur le Maire's full attention."

"'So,' said Madeleine, 'the authorities have their man. What a relief to all good citizens of France. Women and children—and our country's apple orchards—can now rest secure. Does that end the tale, then? Our town's business presses upon me.'"

"'No, Monsieur. I have additional details. Both you and Champmathieu share the same year of birth. Without doubt, we have in custody at last the scofflaw, Jean Valjean.' Charles, I had my long-sought archenemy within my grasp."

"What a relief, Javert. How did Madeleine respond to this news?"

"With annoying calmness. I had more to add. 'Today, I received a personal summons to affirm the man's identity. Thus my confession to you, Honorable Mayor. I have done grievous damage to your reputation, by exposing you to unmerited harm at the hands of the gendarmerie and the courts. I beg your forgiveness and resign myself to dismissal from the township's police service.' What do you think of that, Charles?"

"Oh my, Javert, surely that summons caused you great personal suffering. I find your desire to resign most honorable."

"Correct. I expected immediate dismissal from his presence and my post."

"'What action did the Mayor take against you?"

"He queried me further about Champmatieu, asking what this

man… the former convict… had to say for himself? 'Of course,' I responded, 'the wimp denied everything, claiming no knowledge of anyone called Jean Valjean.'"

*   *   *

"Javert, I have little experience of criminal justice. Does it ever happen that a witness gives false testimony against a suspect to achieve some reciprocal benefit from a magistrate?"

"Certainly, Charles, but not in the case at hand. I alone had firsthand experience with this Valjean fellow. If they arrested the wrong man, I better than any other would know.

"I left by coach at dawn to arrive at Arras just after the midday recess. What greater joy than to testify against that criminal, my nemesis. In doing so, I hoped to turn the key in Jean Valjean's final prison cell. No gift from God or honor bestowed by the State filled me with more pride and pleasure than the prospect of having my moment of delayed triumph. My final vindication."

"In what temper did the Mayor receive this news?"

"He betrayed neither joy nor alarm. I have never known a man so capable of revealing nothing in his facial expression and posture. He remained silent, deep in thought before saying, 'You have cause to rejoice despite your erroneous accusation about my identity.'

"'Yes, Monsieur Mayor, at last I shall taste the sweet fruit of having the final word.'

"The Mayor paused before adding, 'I have little interest in these details.'

"With that Monsieur Madeleine returned his attention to the affairs of city government. For my part, I did not move. 'Sir, if I may, I would add a final observation.'

"'Yes, Inspector. What else do you have to say?'"

*   *   *

"'Sir, there remains something of which I must remind you.'

"Madeleine breathed a sigh of patient indifference. 'Refresh me.'

"'My post, sir. I urge you to dismiss me. Immediately.'

"Monsieur Madeleine rose from his chair for the first time since I entered his office. I knew not what to expect. Did he intend to strike me? Or wrap a supportive arm around my shoulder? His actual reply came as a shock.

"'Javert, you exaggerate your faults. I do esteem both you and your work. Rather than remove you, I intend to notify the Prefect in Paris that you deserve a promotion. For now, I wish you to retain your post in Montrieul-sur-Mer.'

"Charles, God struck me dumb. I swear it. Recovering my composure, I gazed at Madeleine. 'Monsieur Mayor, I cannot grant you that.' My retort seemed to startle him. He replied with an enigmatic, 'Oh?'

"'I respect you as an honorable man, sir. A respected mayor and a just magistrate. I have upheld the Law against all enemies of France. In doing so, I have treated others severely. I must now treat myself with equal severity.'

"Madeleine offered his outstretched hand and said, 'We shall see.' Charles, I dared not return the gesture."

"Why? Madeleine offered an olive branch. Your match ended in a draw."

"I considered his words a stern rebuff. I stood before him erect. 'In my world, a mayor does not offer his hand to a police spy who abused the power of his office.' With that, I bowed and started for the office door. There, I turned once more to face my superior. 'I shall continue to serve, but only until you have secured a replacement.' With that I exited the Mayor's office."

"And did you, Javert?"

"Did I what, Charles?"

"Resign your office?"

"Quite the contrary. Our beneficent God blessed me with full vindication."

"How did that come about?"

*   *   *

"Madeleine himself saved me."

"From what, Javert?"

"From a lifetime of embarrassment. Let me tell you what I learned about events that took place during and after my court testimony.

"The entire proceeding moved like a lava flow creeping down a forested mountainside devouring everything its path. I swore an oath affirming the testimony of the other witnesses. 'Your honor, the alias, Champmathieu, conceals the identity of the long-sought master criminal, Jean Valjean.' My affirmative testimony sealed a guilty verdict. I rejoiced in the demise of my elusive nemesis, proof that deceivers may enjoy but a limited time of undeserved freedom—even, in this case, ill-gotten respect—before their true nature rises to the surface, branding them forever as living a falsehood.

"Having completed my testimony, I left Arras by return coach satisfied that justice had at last prevailed. My pressing duties in Montreuil-sur-Mer awaited me.

"Unknown to me, Charles, Madeleine too journeyed to Arras later that same day. I learned that, upon arriving at the courthouse, he stood before the judge and affirmed that he, not Champmathieu, owned the despicable name, Jean Valjean. He alone bore the former convict's criminal history. His unsolicited testimony shocked the court and everyone present."

"So, that marked the end of the Javert-Valjean conflict? How strange… tragic… and sad. I assume he will spend the rest of his life in prison. To my last days on Earth I prayed each day at Mass for the bedraggled man upon whom I bestowed our family treasures."

"Charles, you wasted your prayers for that inveterate sinner's conversion. Like too many good but naïve Christians, you gave a wandering beggar-thief far too much credit. Believe me, I wished to heaven the whole Valjean affair had concluded and given me peace of mind."

"The story did not end there?"

"For details of what happened in court in my absence, I relied on second- and thirdhand accounts. To my endless shame and disgust, Satan ground my hopes into dust."

"How did that come about?"

"The court police lacked my knowledge of their prisoner's diabolical machinations."

CHAPTER THE EIGHTH:
SATISFACTION

"**B**efore dawn on the morning following my return from Arras, sounds of thunderous pounding on my residence door roused me from sleep. I dressed quickly and opened to find a dust-covered, out-of-breath court messenger standing on my doorstep. I recognized the man from the day before. He handed me a sealed document from the district attorney. His mission completed, the messenger galloped away. Alone in my sitting room, I read the document:

"'By order of the Honorable Circuit Judge, I the District Attorney of Arras commission Inspector Javert, Chief of Police in the township of Montreuil-sur-Mer, to apprehend on sight the escaped prisoner, one Jean Valjean, alias, Madeleine, Mayor of the above-named district, in the event he should he appear within your jurisdiction. Said Honorable Judge remanded the prisoner to confinement awaiting formal sentencing. At a late hour, said criminal, himself a former convict, escaped and vanished. The court considers his capture of utmost urgency for the imminent danger said escapee represents to the populace dwelling in your region.'

"The signature, date, and official gold seal affirmed its origin and authenticity.

"Recall, Charles, I had no knowledge of what took place following my departure from the courthouse until the courier brought the stunning news of Madeleine's—Javert's—shocking confession and bold escape. Had I stayed in Arras and witnessed the confession, I would have warned the authorities to shackle their prisoner at both the wrists and ankles.

"What trickery had this prison-trained wizard up his sleeve? The court relied on me, the Chief of Police, to find and arrest the escapee, should I find him within the environs of my jurisdiction. Believe me, I blamed myself for not staying longer in Arras."

"Because...?"

"In all of France, I alone knew the escapee well enough to anticipate the chameleon's relentless determination to avoid capture. I'd have made certain he did not get away. Not too late, I hoped, had the authorities in Arras assigned me to execute their warrant. Post haste, I set my mind to the task of tracking our sullied mayor."

*   *   *

"Oh, the symmetry of Divine Providence—how beautiful to behold. Correct, Charles? Of course you agree. Keen intuition told me precisely where to look should Valjean return to my jurisdiction. In the depths of my soul and in company of the angels and saints in heaven, I stood at the doorstep of final vindication."

"Thank you for your candor, Javert."

"Every word I have spoken bears the seal of truth."

"Yet, you arrive here at eternity's threshold with every expectation of eternal damnation. How does that fit the spotless servant of the Law you just described?"

"Sadly, Charles, I deserve to spend eternity in unquenchable fire. Thus my desire to conclude our business here and join Satan as one of his most expert fallen angels. What other judgment should I expect than the fate I brought here from... the other side?"

"You know my role here, Javert, does not include passing judgment on you. Far from it. Let me say this from my own experience on Earth and since my arrival in Afterlife. Probity, sincerity, candor, conviction, a sense of duty—each of these virtues has a countering dark side which masks some underlying untruth."

"Of what untruth do you speak?"

"A canceling vice casts a shadow on every virtue. On Earth I called it... 'the evil of the good.'"

"Thus, the need for law and order in society—and in what you, Charles, call Afterlife as well, I'm sure."

*   *   *

"Charles, I knew better than anyone what motivated our fallen Mayor. He would not disappear forever. Nor leave France for Britain, Switzerland, Italy, or the Americas. He did not think as other desperate men do. And I, better than any living being, understood the imposter's unique mentality. Clever… shrewd… fearless. Willing to risk capture in order to clean up his messes.

"I expected Valjean to return to say his goodbyes. First on his list… that slut, Fantine. Immediately, I charted a plan to set a trap around the hospital. I had word even before this day that the woman lay close to death in the care of the good but naïve Sisters of Charity. Knowing Valjean as I did, he would not disappear without first assuring her safety… or seeing to her burial."

"You knew him that well, Javert?"

"Intimately."

"Did you find him at the hospital?"

*   *   *

"I did, Charles. I did indeed."

"And you enjoyed that moment of personal vindication."

"One would think so, but—Trust me, no encounter with Jean Valjean ever concluded as calculated."

"Javert, I must say your narrative holds me in suspense. I await the outcome of this confrontation with the man you refer to as your most despised enemy."

"To ensure the success of my plan, I requisitioned the nearby army post for the assistance of a corporal and four armed soldiers. The rising sun had not yet crept over the eastern horizon. Thus, we had the advantage of darkness. Arriving at the hospital courtyard, I ordered my men to remain alert and out of sight at the four corners of the building.

"I showed them a rough sketch of my prey and issued a stern command, a warning. 'Whatever you do, watch carefully. If this man enters the hospital grounds—or tries to leave, do not approach him. Instead, shoot... to kill.'

"Next, I rang for the portress and asked in an even voice, 'Good Sister, would you kindly point the way to Fantine's room. I received word she has suffered a turn and wish to visit her for a moment. I shall not stay long.'

"I searched her eyes and mouth for a telling twitch. Instead, she expressed not the slightest alarm at my pre-dawn arrival."

"Entering the building, I caught sight of Valjean as he mounted the stairs. Had I not known better I might have thought he possessed not a care in the world. Just an ordinary man on his way to the bedside of a dying friend. Or did she mean more to him than that? A great deal more, in my estimation.

"Careful not to make a sound, I too ascended the stairs. Arriving at Fantine's chamber I turned the handle, eased the door open with the silence of a monk—or spy—and entered. I stood erect in the half-open door, hat on my head, one hand thrust into the chest of my heavy black coat. In the bend of my elbow rested the leaden head of my walking stick, most of which lay tucked out of sight behind me. I cannot count the heads I cracked with that serviceable weapon. Thus I remained for a full minute without a soul perceiving.

"I had not seen Fantine since the day the mayor ripped her from my grasp. Of a sudden, the dying woman raised her clouded eyes. They grew wider when she saw me and struggled to comprehend the danger I represented. Her failing life force revealed a flight response, as if Satan himself stood at her side poised to whisk her away to the Hell she deserved for her life of sin and degradation.

"This, of course, alerted Madeleine—Valjean—to follow her gaze. In silence, he studied my granite features and attire. Oh, the heavenly satisfaction, Charles! The joy of at last having the notorious Jean Valjean in my clutches. A bottomless rage born of past encounters surged within me, along with memories of the humiliation I suffered in the stationhouse, in full view and hearing of my officers. I dared not allow that man to best me a second time.

"Standing now openly before him, I congratulated myself for accurately divining our imposter mayor's true identity, long before anyone else. Fitting for the shrewdest officer on any police force in France. In that moment of ultimate victory, a sunburst glow filled both body and mind. The glory of my triumph overflowed. I ascended to the most gratifying moment in my entire career.

"Justice. Diligence. Absolute commitment to truth. All my virtues intertwined, clothing me in that one delicious moment of conquest. This state of unaccustomed euphoria affirmed my God-given calling to pulverize evil within and around me. I gloried in the triumph of authority, right reason, final judgment… an Easter resurrection of legal conscience and public prosecution.

"I, Inspector Javert, had kept my vow to protect the right order of the government. I played a major role in enforcing the Law by summoning its most potent lightning bolts. I had spent my life avenging threats to decent society. I saw my vocation as lending a helping hand to the Supreme Judge, from whom all divinely appointed judges received their authority. In that one glorious moment, I stood erect in the light of human and divine glory. This victory affirmed my lifelong state of righteousness in society's mortal combat against evil.

"I had spent my entire career tramping my foot upon the slimy reptiles of vice, rebellion, and perdition, each with its own plague to loose upon the earth. My body glowed with the inner radiance of Saint Michael, God's most proficient Archangel. I earned my ultimate reward for doing battle with Satan and his diabolical influence on the great unwashed masses of my sacred and beloved France.

"Divine vindication! Nothing sweeter existed in this world than to learn that I alone, that false Mayor's appointed Chief of Police— among all the wise and seasoned officers of both police and court— knew in my bones what ruses this criminal might unleash."

"Still, Javert, one fact remains. You erred in siding with the false witnesses against the innocent Monsieur Champmathieu."

"To my eternal shame."

"How do you explain such a mistake?"

"It shames me to admit that… for the first time in my career,

Charles—the shameful words stick in my throat—I lost focus amid the trial's pageantry and drama. Not to mention my blind, justice-driven desire to drop the final curtain on Jean Valjean's life of crime and prolonged flaunting of the Law."

*   *   *

"Tell me more about your caper at the hospital."

"As I said, I stood tall and erect in the open doorway, blocking the only path of escape. Charles, everything I had worked for culminated in this one moment of utter and thrilling triumph.

"The satisfaction of at last ensnaring the despised Jean Valjean filled me with pride and fulfillment. The humiliation of having lost the scent and slipping into the error of falsely identifying Champmathieu carved a deep wound in my pride. I took refuge in having at last accurately divined the true criminal hiding beneath a mayoral disguise.

"May I go so far as to boast that I tasted the glory of heaven in that moment? A strange thing to say now that I—society's bastion of protection against chaos and disorder—myself stand at the gates of Hell.

"Jean Valjean then uttered something, Charles, I never expected to hear in my lifetime."

"Oh?"

"Standing at the bedside of that fallen woman, he took her limp hand in his and spoke directly to me… 'Javert, I wish to thank and compliment you for taking time from your busy life to testify at poor Champmatieu's trial.'

"Immediately, my mind sought to identify the malevolent ruse he had plotted. 'I did… my sworn duty… as always,' I stammered.

"I had not seen Fantine since the day the mayor ripped her from my grasp. Her failing life force revealed a fright response, as if Satan himself stood at her bedside ready to whisk her away to the Hell she deserved for her life of sin and degradation. She feared I had come to reclaim her, even as she felt the remaining seconds of her life drip away. She hid her face in both hands and shrieked, 'Monsieur Madeleine, save me!'

"The imposter she knew only by his most recent alias leaned close to her ear. In a surprisingly gentle but audible voice, he whispered, 'Do not excite yourself, dearest Fantine. He has not come for you.' Then, calmly, he turned to address me, 'I know what you want, Javert.'

"'Aware of Valjean's greater strength and prowess I dared not advance more than a few paces. 'I order you, scum! Come with me. Soldiers surround this building waiting to escort you to prison.'

"Fantine shrieked, 'Monsieur Mayor!'

"I burst out laughing. 'No mayor here, woman! Just a thief and deceiver of honest citizens.'

"'No, Inspector, you—' A fit of coughing interrupted her defense.

"Valjean breathed a commanding, 'Javert—'

"'Inspector to you, 24601!'

"'Monsieur,' Valjean continued in a lowered voice, 'May I speak with you in private.'

"'Whatever you have to say, I want her to hear every word of it.'

"After a moment's hesitation he whispered. 'I have one request. You alone should hear it.'

"'A favor! You deserve not a gram of consideration.'

"'Grant me just three days' grace.'

"I surged forward and twisted his collar in my fist. 'Did you not hear me?'

"'I must fetch the child of this unhappy woman from the Thenardiers. I will bring her here to remain under the care of the good Sisters. Accompany me there and back if you choose.'

"'You think me a fool? You mean three days during which to escape my clutches forever! For what? To fetch this harlot's bastard child? You have lost your mind.'

"Suddenly, a second fit of coughing and tremors seized Fantine. 'My child! …Cosette… rescue my child… I want my child…'

"'Hold your tongue, hussy! Monsieur Madeleine does not exist. He never existed. This confessed criminal cannot save you—or your child.'

"Struggling to breathe, she dared to counter between bouts of chest-rattling wheezes, 'Never did... a mother... give life to a... greater saint than... Monsieur Madeleine's.'

"'This man you canonize has exposed himself as no more than a common thief, a brigand and escaped convict. His birth name? Jean Valjean! And now I have him in my grasp. His next stop? Prison for the rest of his useless life.'

"Fantine raised herself in bed and gazed first at Valjean then at me and the attending nun who had slipped into the room in response to the dying woman's cries. Fantine opened her mouth as though to speak but stopped. A rattle rose from the depths of her diseased chest. As if drowning, she stretched out her arms in rigid agony pleading for rescue. In the next instant, she fell back onto her pillow. The back of her skull struck the headboard with a dull thud and fell forward onto her wasted breasts.

"Valjean used a free hand to loosen my grip. I had no power against his superior strength. 'You murdered this woman, Javert,' he blubbered through self-induced tears.

"'March! My armed cohort awaits us in the courtyard. Come quietly if you care for the safety of the holy women who staff this hospital. I can shut down this disease-infested building any time I wish.'

"I had not noticed until this moment a dismantled iron bedframe lodged in a corner of the shadowed room. Valjean stepped away and grabbed one of its iron rods. Turning to face me, he waved it like a bludgeon, his eyes beastlike yet icy and controlled. On assessing his advantage, I retreated a few steps towards the door. Armed with the makeshift weapon, Valjean moved slowly back to Fantine's bed. 'Javert, I advise you not to disturb me at this moment.'

"I considered the situation and retreated further. Why had I not called for my cohorts to enter the hospital? Another uncharacteristic error on my part.

"After hovering over Fantine's motionless body, Valjean bent and cupped her head in one hand. He lowered her gently onto the pillow. He smoothed her hair back under her cap. That done, he pressed his lips to her hand. Valjean then let his makeshift weapon fall to the floor and addressed me with a calmness I found admirable, under the circumstances. 'Now, Inspector Javert, I stand at your disposal.'

"I handcuffed him and led him down the stairs. Having reinforcements at hand guaranteed a successful transfer of our prisoner to the head jailer. Thus assured, I marched my prize straight to the city prison."

*   *   *

"'Javert, where did you go? You drifted away."

"Forgive me. I lost myself in the memory of that apex moment. I tell you, Charles, I felt more elated than at any time in my career… in my life."

"What happened next?"

"I had closed the prison door on a case that remained open far too long. Next, I would send a courier to the Magistrate at Arras to share the news that I had captured the wily escapee. Another feather in my cap, so to speak."

"And now, Javert?"

"It all seems… how can I say it? Of no great matter. …Did I truly just say that?"

"You did."

"How could the quest of a lifetime seem in retrospect so… insignificant?"

"As you now understand, Javert, things appear different when viewed from the perspective of your current state of being. If you had an opportunity to relive that moment now, how might you change the outcome? Or would you?"

"Let me confess to you, Charles, something I never admitted to anyone before. In that deathbed scene, I saw for the first time in Valjean's tender words and actions… genuine love."

"You have so much to learn here, my son—"

"Do not call me your 'son,' Charles! I never identified myself as anyone's son. I arrived in this world by some accident of fate and sinful passion. A whore's disastrous coupling with a thief and no-count wretch judged unfit to mix with honorable society. Only with

Satan's cohorts. They have preceded me into the unquenchable furnace, I suppose. Who could have surmised my destiny to join them? May our wretched souls never meet in Hell. I, Inspector Javert, will see to it that we never meet."

"I know not how to ease your suffering, Javert."

"You cannot. Furthermore, I neither ask nor want your sympathy. May we please finish this review. You torment me as if I already bake in that oven."

"Since you wish to conclude this review, let's proceed. But first, return to that hospital scene. Fantine had just passed from the world of the living."

"Yes. Fantine appeared in the moment of death, dare I say... angelic. Discounting the presence of her discredited mayor, she died alone... as I did. Yes, alone, in a world that offered her no solace. My lust for the glory of returning Valjean to the galleys blinded me to all she had suffered. In that instant—if I may reveal my most closely held secret—I envied them."

"Valjean too?"

"Can you believe it? For the first time since casting my lot with divinely sanctioned enforcers of law and order, I felt... shame."

"You surprise me, Javert. Describe for me your experience of shame."

"Disgrace... for indulging a common weakness of human nature. I had lived my life in rectitude from boyhood when I ran errands for the prison warden. In all my subsequent years, I allowed no space for moral complexities. Yet, here in your presence, Charles, it all seems so... dare I admit it... meaningless. Why? Can you answer me that?"

"I can, Javert, but I question your readiness to receive a truthful response. With Jean Valjean in your grasp, I expect the rest of your story to chart a path to triumph and praise from your superiors, even promotion to Prefect of Paris."

"It shames me to tell you the rest of my story, but I see I must, before you hand me over to the Prince of Darkness."

CHAPTER THE NINTH:
FOILED AGAIN

"**A**fter securing Valjean in a doubly guarded cell, I made my way to my residence. In the early evening small groups gathered on street corners. Walking through the now-safe streets of Montreuil-sur-Mer, I gloried as the great general, Julius Caesar, must have following a glorious triumph over the Gallic tribes. I allowed myself a moment of deep inner satisfaction, allowing even the barest slit of a smile in reward for my success. I had achieved the prime goal of my lifetime.

"I no longer needed elevation to the highest rank of my profession. I measured my professional success and, yes, even my personal satisfaction, by at last putting that slippery convict away in my jail, until I could transport him to a permanent prison. Before leaving the stationhouse, I warned my men to guard him at risk of expulsion from the force, perhaps even loss of their own freedom. How different a fate Valjean would experience in my city prison. As I mentioned earlier, I no longer feared a fiasco similar to the travesty at Arras.

"No one approached me directly of course, but the town at eventide buzzed with news and wild rumors. As I strode by, head erect, my face a stone carving, I caught patches of whispered conversations as word of their former Mayor's arrest and jailing spread from citizen to citizen.

"'Have you heard? Can you believe? Our Mayor a paroled convict!'

"'Monsieur Madeleine?'

"'The same.'

"'You're sure?'

"'They're saying he pulled that fake name out of a hat. His never-known given name has a frightful sound, something like Bejean, or Bonjean, Boujean.'

"'Good God! How did we let him betray us with such a ruse?'

"At another corner, a group of men gathered. I heard one say, 'Has our brave Chief of Police truly locked that beast away in our city prison? If so, our wives and children will rest easy tonight.'

"'I have it on good authority. He rots in custody as we speak, thanks to our diligent Chief.'

"'In our own city prison?' asked another citizen.

"'Yes, I hear tomorrow they'll hand him over to the court in Arras. From there, the filthy bastard will transfer to a secure, escape-proof prison.'

"I passed another group of huddled men and overheard one of them speculate, 'It appears they'll try him for a highway robbery committed long ago. Can you imagine, he stole money from an innocent boy?'

"'A child? Thank heaven our children no longer need to fear.'

"'I suspected as much. I kept it to myself because no one would listen. I always thought the man a bit too perfect. Some evil history lurked behind all that perfection. He bestowed a few coins on any unworthy scamp he came across. Little did they know he might pick their pockets to retrieve his coins before sending them off.'

"And so it went. In truth I admit, Charles, I gloried in these accolades, glowed with pride over my vindication. I had reached the pinnacle of my professional life. At last, the imposter who called himself Madeleine in our town would vanish from Montrieul-sur-Mer."

"So then, Javert, the whole town, including those who once earned a decent living in the former mayor's button factory, turned on their formerly beloved employer."

"Only a handful of fools in all the town remained faithful to the memory of their safely jailed imposter mayor."

"So many people out of work, Javert. Had you no pity for them?"

"Their own misfortune, Charles, for casting their lot with the devil, known or unknown. Valjean got what he deserved. So did his employees. The next day, I would close the factory and bolt the carriage gate shut."

"And Fantine? Did she get a proper burial?"

"I left that to the hospital Sisters. I expect they laid her, as deserved, in an unmarked pauper's plot."

"End of story, Javert?"

"I prayed on the heads of every saint in heaven that we had slammed the door, not only on his factory but on that man's freedom... his life."

"Hmm. I sense your story might yet have at least one more chapter."

"Astute, Charles. It pains me to admit this. I had not yet written 'The End' after the last chapter in the life of criminal Jean Valjean."

"Continue, then. I cannot wait to hear the next episode in your Book of Life."

*   *   *

"Late on the same night of my first day of glory and relief... word came that the impossible had occurred. ...Valjean had escaped. I raced to see for myself, only to find an empty cell!"

"How did that come about, Javert? After your diligent precautions—"

"One of the two officers posted outside his cell took a latrine break; the other dozed off in his chair. The liars swore they lapsed for, as they pleaded, 'No more than a minute... maybe two... three at most.'

"Valjean's legendary strength exceeded that of any man alive. No other could bend those old and apparently loosening bars at the window. Except Jean Valjean. I blamed myself. I had witnessed how he saved a man trapped beneath a huge fallen boulder."

"Yes, at Toulon you told me, Javert. Also in Montreuil-sur-Mer, when a wagon wheel broke loose from a loaded cart pinning a townsman surnamed Fauchlevant underneath. When no one offered help, including yourself, Madeleine pushed everyone aside and, like a human jack, lifted the wagon, enabling bystanders to pull the injured man free."

"Correct, Charles."

"Oh my. I had no idea. When I encountered him in Digne, he seemed barely able to stand, let alone perform such a feat."

"With due respect, you did not know Valjean as I knew him."

"Pardon me, Javert, for interrupting your narrative. Please, finish your recollection of the events of the day you discovered Valjean's escape."

"Why had I not posted an extra patrol outside the wall beneath his cell window? A stupid mistake for any experienced officer of the law and certainly for a Chief of Police. I had given myself permission to gloat in the man's capture and jailing within one of my own—I mistakenly deemed—escape-proof cells…"

*   *   *

"You have gone quiet again, Javert."

"Failing to outthink the escapee, I set about recapturing him. I went directly to his residence where a portress blocked my way.

"'My good sir,' said she, 'I have not exited the house all day. Not once. I swear to you by our all-seeing God, Monsieur Madeleine has not entered this house, not during the day… or this night.'

"With this, I knew she had willfully committed the heinous crime of lying to an officer of the law. I shoved her aside when I spied an open window at the top of the stairs."

"'I opened it,' she volunteered.

"Another lie. I made a mental note to deal with this old bag in due time. The business at hand outweighed her lesser but duly noted offences. I ascended the stairs to find Valjean's chamber door slightly ajar. Rushing into the room truncheon in hand, I found an old nun on her knees, eyes shut tight, praying some gibberish. There I stood amid two terrified women but no Valjean. I hesitated to enter the room further."

"Why, Javert?"

"I hold nuns in special veneration. 'Sister,' I said, 'are you alone in this room?'

"She raised her tear-filled eyes. 'Yes.'

"'Then, you will excuse me if I persist. My duty binds me to ask. Have you seen a certain person—a man—this evening? An escaped criminal. Certainly, you know of whom I speak.'

"'Monsieur Madeleine?'

"'Allow me to inform you I have learned that man's true name. Valjean. Jean Valjean. He fooled many people here, masquerading as Mayor Madeleine. Do you swear on your veil that you have not seen him this day or last night?'

"The sister ceased her weeping. 'I have not.'

"'Then I beg your forgiveness for frightening you... and interrupting your prayer.' I bowed deeply, descended the stairs two at a time and left the house to strategize how best to track my elusive escapee."

"And so, my dear Javert, that marked the end of your association with Jean Valjean, alias Monsieur Madeleine?"

"It pleases me, Charles, to tell you I neither closed the case nor shut it down."

CHAPTER THE TENTH:
HOW JAVERT LOST THE GAME

"**D**espite my sullied reputation, I resumed the routine of leading the police in Montreuil-sur-Mer."

"You recovered, then, from your disappointment, losing Jean Valjean's trail."

"No, the events of that day further fueled my resolve. I swore to find and capture that man, see him pay dearly for his crimes. Only in that way might I satisfy my ravenous craving to bury him alive in the dank and putrid belly of a galley ship.

"One week after the events just related, fate smiled upon me—or Divine Providence, as a man of the cloth might prefer. The man I call my patron, Monsieur Chabouillet, now holding the office of Secretary of the Prefecture in Paris, lifted me from my personal prison in Montreuil-sur-Mer to join him as second-in-command in our glorious capital city."

"Quite a promotion considering it came at a dark period in your career."

"The assignment letter commended me for, and I quote, 'rendering unflagging assistance in the ongoing search for France's most wanted criminal, Jean Valjean.' This news brought instant relief. At last, an opportunity to display my unmatched skills on the grandest stage of all."

"I feel your exhilaration, Javert. And your relief."

"And validated for my otherwise spotless career, Charles."

"So, you bade adieu to the whole Jean Valjean affair."

"Immersed in the challenging duties of my new position, that name ceased to haunt me day and night, as before. Until one day in mid-December of that same year. I, who rarely read a newspaper, happened to notice a frontpage article in a week-old edition of the English language *Galignanis Messenger*. I could not read English, but a name leapt out from the bottom of the front page. It captured my immediate and focused attention."

"And that name was?"

"Jean Valjean."

*   *   *

"Charles, I stared at that hated name as memories of my humiliation rampaged within me. Forcing myself to restrain my roiling emotions, I struggled to read further. In essence, the article announced that my nemesis… had died! On that singular day Divine Providence placed that journal in my hand. Any other day I would have missed it and remained unaware of my liberation—or relative freedom, I should say.

"Should I feel elated and shout, 'Wonderful news'? Or keep hope alive that one day I would find him and deliver him in person—in chains this time—to an appointed prison? If the report proved factual, I would forever regret missing the pleasure of consigning that evil man to the Hell he deserved."

"So much hate, Javert. Could you find no pity within your spirit?"

"My career demanded leaving reconciliation to the clergy, like yourself, Charles."

"Forgive the interruption. You own this history. Tell it as you will."

"I decided to accept the report as fact and put my recurring nightmares to rest. I tossed the paper into a trash bin… and breathed a deep sigh. Never again would I allow my long-sought tormentor to invade my daily thoughts or haunt my sleep.

"From that day forward, I immersed myself in my work. At each arrest of a man, woman, or child, I beheld the face of the man I once wanted most to capture. Each surrogate perpetrator found Valjean's rightful place in life—a prison cell or a galley ship. My relief proved temporary."

*   *   *

"Some months later, my successor as Chief of Police at Montreuil-sur-Mer filed a new report with our prefecture in Paris. It concerned a recent abduction of a minor child under what he described as 'peculiar circumstances.' The suspect—hear this well, Charles—fit the broad description of the deceased Valjean. Apparently a woman—the mother—now deceased had entrusted her daughter to the care of an innkeeper of that region. Does that not sound familiar? The report cited the child as the daughter of a woman known as—"

"Fantine. I'm sure, Javert, you had memorized that name and preserved it within your flawless memory."

"Exactly, the same woman who died in my presence in the hospital at Montreuil-sur-Mer the night I arrested Jean Valjean."

"Quite a coincidence."

"The report failed to indicate an exact date but it set my recall in motion. The death scene in the Sisters' hospital stormed back in vivid detail. As she lay dying, Fantine spoke the child's name—Cosette. I remembered hearing the dying woman beg Valjean to rescue her daughter from an innkeeper by the name of Thenardier. By reputation, himself a shady rascal.

"I strung the pieces in sequence one by one. Valjean must have gone there to find the child. It made perfect sense that such a wizard might fake his own death to throw me off the trail. Now the local police reported her stolen by a stranger. Who else could that refer to than the presumably deceased Jean Valjean?

"It came to me as no shock that the scofflaw had planted his own obituary in a Paris newspaper.

"Without informing anyone about my destination, I took a coach to Montreuil-sur-Mer. And from there by horseback to the scene of the crime in a nearby village.

"Upon my arrival, the grief-stricken proprietor, Thenardier, chattered on about their shared sorrow, relating how their 'beloved little Lark' had gone missing. Expecting to gather a firsthand report about the crime from the Thenardiers, I found only obscurity awash with a torrent of bald-faced lies.

"I spent the rest of the day interviewing villagers who offered spicy descriptions of the Thenardier family. By day's end, I had gathered a variety of alternate versions of the story. Each ended with the abduction of the minor child. Hence the police report. I sensed immediately that Monsieur Thenardier had sought pity from his neighbors. Instead, he aroused the curiosity of the regional prosecutor. I recalled the ancient proverb: 'Owls shun candlelight.'

"Clearly, Innkeeper Thenardier had forbidden his wife to speak during my inquiry. According to her husband, having that dear little creature 'ripped from her bosom' had broken this surrogate mother's heart, rendering her incapable of speaking about the matter.

"Most damning of all, the innkeeper could not explain why he had received in recompense one thousand five hundred francs from the dastardly 'kidnapper.'

"Late that same afternoon, I returned to Paris."

*   *   *

"What conclusion did you draw from your visit to the grieving family?"

"I declared myself a ninny for hoping the whole affair had any connection to Valjean."

"And thus concluded—again—your *affaire* Valjean."

"So I thought. Until March in the year of Our Lord 1824. By then three years had passed."

"What happened?"

"Word reached me through my network of informants and spies concerning a certain person who dwelt in a shabby Paris neighborhood of Saint-Medard. Locals knew this stranger not by name but only as 'the mendicant who gives alms.'

"According to gossip on the street, locals knew the unnamed man as a respectable person of some means. No one knew his given name, which he never offered. The story went that he lived alone with a little girl of eight to ten years, who knew nothing about herself, other than her place of birth—"

"Montreuil-sur-Mer."

"The very same. I had an informer on my payroll in the neighborhood of the sighting. An old beggar. On occasion, this vagabond served me as a second pair of eyes. He told me about a similar experience with the same gentleman. He described him as one 'quite shy and always wearing the same horrible yellow frockcoat.' My informer added that this mystery man appeared only after sundown and spoke to no one except the poor.

"Needless to say, this piqued my curiosity. To get a firsthand look at this phantasmic gentleman without alarming him, I donned a church beadle's outfit and went to the place where I might find the man on most evenings."

"I cannot wait to hear more, Javert."

"Well, Charles, as Providence would have it, the same individual did indeed approach me, coin in hand. At that moment, I raised my head. A jolt of recognition ripped through me. I swear this man had the same reaction on coming face to face with me.

"On later reflection that evening, I suffered grave doubts. Darkness and shadows might have misled me. Besides, as I described earlier, according to the press, Jean Valjean had died. You see, Charles, caution guides a professional policeman. I say that considering the spotlight of Parisian political sensitivity. Since arriving in the capital I never laid a finger on a suspect unless absolutely certain about the identification.

"Instead, I followed the man to a tenement called Corbeau House. As an experienced professional in the fine art of criminal investigation, I knew how to get the portress talking. The old woman confirmed—how accurately I knew not—she had once seen thousand franc notes in my prey's possession! I proceeded to hire a room and listened at the mysterious lodger's door, hoping to catch the sound of his voice, but he and the child spoke only in indecipherable whispers."

*　　　　*　　　　*

"The following evening, I spotted my suspect emerging from his quarters. I followed and took cover behind a row of trees lining the boulevard. With me, I had two officers recruited from the Prefecture of the Rue de Pontoise. I kept the man's name to myself, in the event my identification of the wealthy almsgiver proved faulty."

"Javert, I confess to ignorance of the inner workings of law enforcement, but did you not risk losing him again in the city's crowded lanes and byways?"

"Yes, the slightest indiscretion might put my prey on high alert. In the end, the exquisite glory of unveiling him drove me to proceed. I took each step with utmost caution. Imagine the shame raining down on me if I arrested someone I misidentified as a man previously and publicly pronounced deceased!"

"I agree with your caution, Javert. I do."

"A single erroneous judgment might jeopardize the stellar reputation I'd earned during my decades-long career. Yet, as the story unfolded, Charles, I should have followed my professional instinct."

"You lost him?"

"As I said, the Parisian environment at that time had turned against the more aggressive tactics of the police. The press had only recently exposed our prefecture—not me—for a number of high profile arrests that proved, shall I say, arbitrary. The negative effects reached as far as the Chamber of Deputies, which at that time frowned upon interference with what they cited as 'individual liberties.' To falsely arrest a grandfather out walking with his juvenile granddaughter. ...Well, you can imagine the uproar."

"I see how that night might have detoured quite badly for you."

*   *   *

"I had the upper hand and maintained complete control. I knew my suspect better than any officer of the law. Not only a disguised escapee with the cunning of a fox but slippery as cobblestones newly iced over. I followed my flawless instinct, out of sight but ever close to the kidnapper and child. I trailed the mystery pair to the Pont d'Austerlitz, which, as you know, connects one bank of the Seine to the other. I approached the tollkeeper, 'Have you seen an older man walking with a little girl?'"

"'*Oui, monsieur.*'

"Just then, I spied my mouse traversing an illuminated spot on the other side of the river. With him, hand in hand, I saw the minor child. Unwittingly, that master of disguise entered the Cul-de-Sac Genrot. I dispatched one of my officers to guard that location and requisitioned a passing patrol.

"With these lookouts in position, I used my experience and cunning to trap the pair between a blind alley on the right and my agent on the left. I possessed in that moment such confidence and exhilaration I paused and allowed myself a celebratory pinch of snuff. My only vice."

"So, you had every confidence of catching them in your trap and interrogating both man and child?"

"Exactly. With the game begun, we tightened the net until we maneuvered the pair into a high-walled, dead-end lane. I advanced slowly and in silence."

"So, you had the man you believed the true Jean Valjean and the missing child, Cosette, firmly in your grasp."

"So I reckoned. When I…"

"Why do you hesitate?"

"When I reached the center of the web, poof! The mouse had vanished. Imagine my exasperation. Why had I not nailed him when I had him within arm's reach? Whatever my failure in the moment, I did not give up. I spent the night exploring residential gardens and dark alleyways alone. In addition, I established sentinels and organized other traps and ambush points. With the exception of a cloistered convent, we searched every square meter of the area the whole night long.

"At daybreak, I faced the dreary reality that I had lost the proverbial needle in my own haystack. But how to retrieve that needle? I returned to the Prefecture of Police feeling defeated and shamed. Imagine! A police spy ensnared by his prey."

"And so, Javert, that ended your search for the elusive Jean Valjean?"

"In truth, Charles, for the first time ever I admitted defeat. How could the God of Justice, for whose noble cause I daily risked life and limb, so cruelly deny me the pleasure of one day finding Valjean alive? And the satisfaction of bringing him to justice?"

*   *   *

"I never stopped searching for my most hated enemy but only in the privacy of my ever-alert mind. Each day thereafter, I studied the eyes of every adult male meeting his general description. A fruitless endeavor. Never since the creation of man did anyone hope, as I hoped, the day would come when the God of justice would reward my virtue and diligence by letting me find that wizard of disguise."

"I see, Javert, how Valjean's shadowy escape cast a cloud over your life."

"It did... until eight long years had passed into history."

"Are you telling me fate brought you and Valjean face to face again?"

"Must I continue, Charles? Can I not admit to my sins and enter my inevitable destination? Hell's fires cannot cause me more suffering than revisiting my most horrid mistake in minute detail."

CHAPTER THE ELEVENTH:
A MAN RECRUITED

"**I** cherish not what lies in wait, Charles. Can you offer me no path toward early termination?"

"Though you find this process tortuous in the extreme, my son, what has begun must play itself out in full. If I could, I would spare you these painful admissions of personal and professional failure. Uncountable souls preceded you. A star-filled universe of others will follow."

"Why do you insist on calling me your 'son'?"

"I claim each of God's children as my own child."

"Clearly, you have hit upon what separates us, Charles. I had no human son, no brother or sister to care about. I made it a point in life never to cultivate friendships. I devoted myself body and soul, just as you did, to serve the Divine One who, in the blistering sands of the Sinai Desert, gave Moses the Ten Commandments carved in stone. Yahweh God commanded the prophet to teach the Israelites the true meaning of Law, Order, and Duty. Foregoing all human relationships, I vowed with singleness of mind to remove from law-abiding society every man, woman and—yes—child steeped in a life of sinful crime. That vow fueled my service, my calling, to the end of my days. At which time, I expected—foolishly, I now understand—to receive an eternal reward for my fidelity to Law, both divine and human."

"Such a lonely existence your Earth life, dear brother."

"I object first to your use of 'lonely.' Also to calling me 'brother'… or for that matter any term of intimacy."

"Surely, you made an exception for your sworn officers in uniform."

"Wrong again. In my vocation, Charles, you trust no one, not your superiors, nor your equals in rank, and not those who serve under your command. One day, I might find sufficient cause to arrest and charge any one of them. With the same determination, I expect you to unlock for me the gates of Hell. I shall gladly throw myself into its eternal flames, yes without reluctance, my head held high."

"That remains to play out. For now, Javert, I invite you to pick up the narrative wherever you wish."

*   *   *

"Without another word or sighting of Jean Valjean, I turned my attention to the daily business of policing the over-crowded metropolis of Paris. With my fervor deepening with each new day, I kept law-abiding citizens safe from vermin—miscreants who crawl from the sewers under cover of night. Until..."

"Until?"

"My last day of Earth life."

*   *   *

"As night fell over Paris on June 6, 1832, a shredding cloud passed across the moon providing a thin blanket of camouflage. With rumors of something nefarious brewing in the streets and alleyways around Rue Des Billettes, I prowled in search of trouble.

"Charles, in all of France, no police spy possessed my skill at blending into the masses. Dressed in the garb of an ordinary working class citizen, I employed my keen instinct for sniffing out trouble. In the vicinity of rue Saint-Martin and rue Saint-Denis, I spotted a hastily constructed barricade blocking one of the city's narrow streets.

"The structure, if one might call it that, consisted of old mattresses, broken tables and chairs, along with miscellaneous pots and pans. Dead bodies ripped from graves? Nothing would surprise me. With haste, I passed my findings to the local military garrison, which made haste to organize a response.

"An hour later, from my hiding place I heard outbursts of comingled voices emanating from behind the barricade. Shots rang out… but at scattered intervals. At what target? A mirage? No opponent had yet arrived to challenge them. Put a gun in the hands of a novice and who can resist the temptation to fire it?

"The source of this activity? Clearly, a ragtag band of foolish, undisciplined amateurs. What in the name of God Almighty did they expect to accomplish? That other Parisian idiots would rise up and join their hopeless crusade to overthrow our monarch and mighty government? By all reports, the city remained calm, except in this ill-chosen death trap.

"As if on cue, a brigade of professional soldiers and their deadly cannons moved into position at the far end of the deserted street. They assembled to launch a sustained charge if the idiots insisted on battle. This respite told me the commander felt no largescale danger and, therefore, no need to rush the inevitable outcome. Soon enough, that band of foolhardy traitors would absorb the slaughter they deserved.

"With the military in place, I determined my best service consisted of finding a way to infiltrate the rebel band, or any name by which they identified themselves. From a dark and secluded alleyway, I entered unseen into the taproom of what had once served as an alehouse full of boisterous celebrants. It appeared to serve as the rebels' ad hoc command post. I seated myself at a dimly lighted corner table and blended into the scene.

"Finding a musket nearby, I took a seat and held the weapon between my legs barrel up as if I had arrived as another brave volunteer eager to risk my life for their as yet unspecified cause. Once the shooting started, I intended to slip out by the same path I used to enter. Then, I planned to signal our troops to block the rebels' only possible escape route. To my surprise, as the room filled with rebel fighters no one questioned my presence among them.

"A visual assessment confirmed my initial judgment. A band of foolhardy, inexperienced recruits consisting of university students joined by a sprinkling of older men and women of the working class. Angry volunteers one and all. Insane dreamers, pitting their misled ideals against the insurmountable force of a French army brigade. For a time I would remain safely behind the barricade, plotting whatever misinformation I might pass to their schoolboy leaders.

"As I constructed my plan, a shifty-eyed boy, looking every bit the part of a thief and pickpocket, entered the tavern. He paid no attention to my presence. I recognized the scruffy lad from somewhere. But where?

"Of a sudden, the lad fixed his gaze on me. In that instant, we identified each other. The youngest Thenardier. What did they call him? Ah yes, Gavroche. A dry limb fallen at the feet of his criminal father. As the little rogue approached, I slid my finger to the musket's trigger. Unaware that I observed his every move, he stole closer allowing me an occasional glance to read his eyes. The boy clenched both fists, opened them, and clenched them again. His whole being set to work, relying on instinct to arrive at an identification. I watched as he rummaged through his puny brain to recall where we had encountered each other and how I happened to count among his rebel companions.

"A tall young man entered the tavern. 'Here you are, little man. I have a job for you. You're small. They might not see you. I need you to go out of the barricade. Slip along close to the buildings. Gather some information about our opponents, their numbers and weaponry.' He gripped the boy's shoulders with both hands. 'When you've sized things up, come back and report what awaits us out there.' With that brief commission, he sentenced the young fool to set off on a no-return mission.

"Gavroche raised himself to his tallest posture. 'So, boss, little chaps'r good for something, after all! Trust the little fellows. Distrust the big ones.' With that he lowered his voice and gestured in my direction. 'See that big fellow over there?'

"'What about him?'

"He whispered but I read his lips… 'police spy.'

"His boss turned and truly saw me for the first time. 'You're sure?'

"'Two weeks past he pulled me by my ear off a cornice of the Port Royal. My crime? Sunnin' m'self.'

"A burly longshoreman type stepped close to Enjolras and murmured a few words in a low tone before exiting the room. Within a minute, he returned accompanied by three broad-shouldered fellows. The four positioned themselves at a table behind me, clearly prepared to hurl themselves upon me. I nursed a fervent desire to stay alive until the army vanquished these idealistic amateurs. I also weighed a disturbing probability. Our soldiers might not recognize me in my disguise and, during the heat of battle kill me along with the others. Weighing both outcomes, the odds against my living out the day soared.

"Enjolras approached. 'Your name?'

"At this abrupt query, I burned my gaze deep into their leader's eyes. My adversary appeared to grasp my meaning. I smiled to let him see exactly what I thought of him and his gang of schoolboy soldiers. I wanted him to know that, despite my handicap, he had much to dread from me and our nation's justice system. With fearless gravity, I addressed him. 'Do you not see the foolishness of this whole doomed affair? If you had any brains at all, you would send your cohorts home to their mothers.'

"'So, you admit to your role as a spy?'

"Intending to throw him off his game, I folded my arms to project a fearless calm. 'I serve as a senior agent of the Paris police.'

"'Your name?' he dared to demand.

"To put him on the defensive, I spat at him. At that, Enjolras signaled to the four men behind me. Before I could turn around, they threw me to the floor and pinioned me for a search. They found my round identification card, set between two pieces of thin glass. On one side, my name and rank. On the other, a coat of arms, engraved with the motto, Supervision and Vigilance.

"Enjolras read aloud, 'Javert, Inspector of Police. Signed by the Prefect, one Monsieur Gisquet.'

"They took my pocket watch and purse, which contained several gold pieces. One of Enjolras' thugs spoke up, 'Something's under the watch.'

"At the bottom of my purse, I had concealed a paper in a tiny envelope. Enjolras unfolded the note and read aloud these lines also signed by the Prefect, 'Upon gathering data, Inspector Javert shall determine the extent of treasonous intrigue and report back.'

"The muscle men lifted me to my feet, bound my arms behind my back, and fastened me with ropes to a round post in the center of the room. Now entwined and immobile, I raised my head with the fearless serenity of a man who had never once in his life told a lie.

"The scamp Gavroche had stayed behind just long enough to witness this sordid scene. With a toss of his head, he approached me, chanting a little ditty, 'So, the rat has caught the cat.'

"All this ensued so rapidly, it ended by the time others positioned outside the wine shop noticed the commotion inside. I uttered not a single cry. Seeing me bound to the post, four other insurrectionists approached their leader. 'Who's this?'

"'A police spy,' Enjolras announced. Turning to me, he pronounced my sentence, 'We will execute you ten minutes before the barricade falls. If it does. Either way, make your peace with God for you shall certainly die this day.'

"So much for my calculated escape. In my most imperious tone, I demanded, 'Why not at once?'

"'We need to ration our powder.'

"'Then finish your evil business with the thrust of a knife,' I demanded.

"'Listen, spy,' Enjolras snarled. 'Honorable men will judge you, not a band of assassins.' He turned to Gavroche, 'Still here? Get on about your business!'

"'I'm going!' the gloating boy answered but halted at the exit and pointed to my now confiscated pistol. 'I'll leave the damn musician with you, but I want his clarinet.'

"'You know your mission. Get to it. You have no need of a gun.'

"With that, the urchin dared to give me a military salute, before dancing gaily out of the inn and, I assumed, slipping through an opening in the barricade."

*   *   *

"I can imagine your quandary, Javert, tied up, unable to help yourself or your army."

"Do I detect a word of compassion, Charles, or do you mock me?"

"I mean no disrespect."

"I employ few words and rely on precise, calculated action. I grow weary retelling my story. Can I not get a pass or whatever leave I need to enter the eternal punishment I merit. Or do you not understand the gravity of my fall from grace? You do recall, Charles, I took my own life."

"Of course I do. With respect, may I remind you that time has no meaning in Afterlife. This process will not delay your desired judgment. So you may carry on, Javert."

"I openly confess to having committed a grave sin against the laws of heaven as they govern the affairs of humankind. I ask no mercy. What more evidence do you need?"

"Many souls in transition bring with them their Earthbound assumptions about God our Father and Afterlife. Believe me, brother, I do understand your reluctance to discuss the scope of your decisions and actions. I admit that too many Christian souls form their expectations based on black-and-white teachings of self-important preachers. In the process, they reduce the crucified Christ to their own level and likeness. Now, Javert, allow me to repeat myself. The rules of transition from life on Earth to Afterlife demand a full review of key moments and decisions made and acted upon over the course of one's life. No one gains exemption."

"No one?"

"Correct."

"What more do you need from me?"

"Not what I desire. Rather, what you need to review. Clearly, your story has not ended."

"Need I relive the bitter end of my earthly life?"

"There exists no other way to complete your transition."

Chapter the Twelfth:
"We Meet Again"

"As the hours passed, I grew impatient with our army's delay. Then, of a sudden, I heard boots striking pavement. I envisioned riflemen and cannons taking positions at the far end of the street. Still they hesitated. Why not mount a charge against this ragtag collection of misfits and malcontents? Had our troops waited for my report before attacking? Or had their overly cautious commander requested reinforcements before hurling his troops onto this pregnable stack of rubble? If so, they overestimated the power of these schoolboy brigands and their assorted hangers on. I cursed the happenstance of Gavroche's recall and accurate identification! Another curse on him for calling me out to his leader.

"Had the army yet to identify the insurgents as no more than a handful of freshly minted lawyers and self-absorbed university students, along with a smattering of laborers and their wives and lovers? In my life, I had never witnessed a more inept collection of untrained boys. They saw themselves as heroes of a new and better France created in their own image and likeness. I hated the rancid odor of them. Even worse, the room wreaked of piss and excrement, yes vomit too. Soon, their blood would add its deathly, suffocating smell to the rest.

"One of the insurgents addressed Enjolras, 'You set on the death of that spy?'

"'I am,' he replied.

"This exchange took place near the post to which they'd bound me. Suddenly, a single rifle shot rang out from the barricade. Aimed at the army's position? From inside the rebel encampment, a man cried out, '*Vive la France!* Long live freedom from tyranny!'

"Another treasonous rebel entered the room. In a quivering voice, he addressed his self-anointed leader, 'They've captured one of our men and executed him.'

"Enjolras glanced toward me. 'Inspector Javert, you will die in compensation for our fallen comrade.'

"I wriggled my wrists, but the one who had bound me knew how to tie a knot. Never had I felt so disadvantaged. I, the master spy and escape artist, could do nothing to prevent my imminent execution."

*   *   *

"Following news of their cohort's death, all abandoned the taproom. Alone at last, I had time to reassess the situation at the barricade. A small contingent of skilled marksmen could wipe this nest of vermin from Paris's sacred streets. Add to that a well-placed cannonball or two. That show of force would bury these rebels' wild fantasies forever amid piles of their own dismembered limbs.

"The tranquility of this brief moment allowed the rebels to assess their odds of survival. In their eyes I read a misguided dream of victory. Soon these young idealists would suffer the apocalypse of civil war.

"In a flash, misguided visions of victory would commingle with fierce clashes and the hopelessness of unimagined defeat... the ultimate failure of their ignoble cause. In the unlikely chance anyone survived, that unfortunate idiot would soon wish he had joined the bloody pile of mates slaughtered in the battle."

"I praise our merciful God, Javert, that I myself never faced a terrifying day such as you describe."

"Then you know not of what I speak, Charles."

"Not firsthand."

"Allow me to continue."

"By all means."

"Corpses pulled from the top of the barricade now lay on crimson cobblestones. These fell in the first volley. But then the army unexpectedly withdrew to their previous position. Had I completed my mission, they would know how little they had to fear. For that, I took full responsibility. My failure necessitated my comrades' hesitation. My spirit sank lower with the turn of each subsequent hour of that eternal night.

"I slid further down the post to which they'd bound me. I lacked leg strength to rise again or track the movement of the sun as it chased darkness from the sky. I counted myself fortunate to see at least one more Parisian day.

"Some hours later, a distant clock tower broke the silence. One, two, three. It completed its cycle. Twelve. Midday. The echo of the bell's final stroke had not passed into the atmosphere before Enjolras entered the wine shop command post.

"Sure of victory, the rebels had left themselves no clear avenue of escape at their rear. Enjolras hurled a thundering order to those outside, 'Carry stones into the shop. Line the windowsills with them. Half the men upstairs with their guns, the other half to the paving stones outside. We've not a minute to waste.'"

*   *   *

"Their leader's command resulted in dozens of dug up paving stones transported to the upstairs room and attic. I visualized the scene on the other side of the barricade. Certain methodical deliberations precede a final attack. After which, lightning strikes. I envisioned a crack squad of miners bearing explosives moving into place for the final onslaught. With military precision, munitions experts would precede our brave infantrymen. Their mission? Demolish the barricade. Behind the miners and munitions men, an attack column—eager, poised. Since before the turn of the century, this effective tactic bore the descriptor, tug-of-war.

"All this would occur with the precision of an expertly choreographed ballet—although, Charles, I never indulged in theatrical frivolities. The rebels' stones against cannons? Rag-tag volunteers against a superbly trained battalion? I inhaled the sweet aroma of a final battle soon to begin. With it, the end of these young fools' delusions of grandeur.

"The rebels had to know their only options consisted of an unimaginable victory… or a take-no-prisoners slaughter. Let other young fools learn this lesson: any such rebellion deserved and could expect no less than complete and swift annihilation. France would never yield to anarchy. What a powerful message the slaughter about to take place would send to other would-be rebels fantasizing future insurrections.

"Suddenly, twin cannons discharged three-kilogram balls against the center of the barrier. Following that, yet another booming round. I envisioned the balls ripping wide breaches ahead of the final assault.

"The rebels next—and most futile—tactic brought the bombardment's survivors inside. They reinforced the streetside window and secured the wineshop entrance with two iron crossbars. They had now established, they thought, a fortress within a fortress. Didn't those young fools understand they had converted the wineshop into their self-prepared crypt?

"To make their situation even worse, the defenders had to ration their diminishing supply of ammunition. Surely, the army commander surmised this. With the rebels thus sealed off, the invaders planned their next move with irritating leisure.

"Apparently, this delay of the inevitable permitted Enjolras to assess the situation as a futile effort to make perfect the utterly imperfect. The rebel chief appeared to have resigned himself to the outcome, his compatriots' imminent deaths. And his own.

"I heard him confide to a puny traitor named Marius, 'I'll give the final orders inside. For your part, remain outside and observe, but from a secure position on the barrier.'

"I recalled that Marius and I, some time ago, shared a moment of common history. He'd arrived at the prefecture to report that his quarters in a tenement building shared a common wall with a band of ne'er-do-wells. He'd overheard them plotting a crime. With assistance from a cadre of policemen trained for this type of raid, I swept the place clean. Now, back to the barricade.

"Enjolras issued his final orders in a curt but profoundly tranquil tone. I confess I found his leadership skills admirable for an amateur—gravely misguided, of course, but admirable.

"'Comrades, my brothers in the cause of liberty, we now count our remaining assets at twenty-six combatants and thirty-four guns. Load the remaining eight and keep them at hand. Swords and pistols in your belts. Twenty men to the barricade. The remaining six to fire on assailants from upstairs through openings in the stones.'

"Enjolras placed a single loaded pistol on the table. Just when I'd begun to hope he'd forgotten me, he turned and addressed me in a steely voice. Our eyes locked in mutual distain, 'I have a plan for you, Inspector Javert. The last man to leave this room, will smash your skull.'

*   *   *

"I pretended not to hear.

"'Right here?' one of the rebels inquired.

"Enjolras answered him, 'I would never mingle this villain's blood with that of our brave and beloved brothers. Behind us at Mondetour Lane stands a wall only four feet high. We have pinioned him well. The last man out will take him there… and kill him.'

"Clearly, Javert, you did not die a prisoner. How did you survive?"

"I remained impassive throughout the leader's declaration of my death sentence. At that moment, a new man, an elderly rebel, entered the room. He wore an ancient uniform I hadn't seen for at least three decades. I almost laughed aloud, until I saw that none of the rebels seemed to know the man.

"The newcomer addressed Enjolras, 'You the commander here?'

"'Yes,' Enjolras replied.

"I read the rebel leader's annoyance that an aged volunteer should appear out of nowhere at this climactic moment of their doomed revolt.

"'I have a request, sir' the newcomer continued.

"'Do you not perceive our crisis here? Go home, old man. As you see, our cause has failed. No one has come to our aid… none but you. And you arrive too late to make a difference. I will not let you die with the rest of us. Go to your family.'

"'I ask that I may—' The intruder glanced at me and pointed. At that same instant, a jolt of recognition pierced my being.

"Impossible! Jean Valjean, alias Monsieur Madeleine and a string of other fake identities, had risen from the dead! How many lives can one villain have? What a devious game our God played, placing me in the role of perpetual loser? Why resurrect that man to torment me in my final hours?"

"I feel your shock and dismay, Javert."

"The worst has yet to come, Charles. Valjean spoke up, his voice clear and calm. 'I ask that I may have the honor of blowing this man's brains out.' Not a hint of, *I've cornered you at last, my lifelong and most bitter enemy*. His tone of voice might have come from one who just volunteered to prepare a meal for Enjolras and his rebel band.

"I fixed my gaze on my executioner. 'Fate indeed, Jean Valjean. You relish having me at so great a disadvantage, do you not?'

"Enjolras calmly reloaded his own rifle. 'Friend, I have no objections. Though I do not know you, your presence here, your calm demeanor and resolve appear genuine.' Then he gave the fateful order. 'Take that pistol from the table, sir. Finish off this accursed spy.'

"Valjean seized the offered pistol and seated himself at one of the tables. A faint click announced he had cocked the gun and knew how to handle a firearm. Charles, I could accept losing a fair duel. The better man would have won. This abrupt and unceremonious end of my storied life offered not a mite of satisfaction. Of a sudden, a blast of trumpets issued from the army's position.

"'Take care!' a spotter cried from the top of the barricade.

"'I recognized that voice. The weasel, Marius Pontmercy. France and the world would soon rid themselves of him. And good riddance, rebel! Suddenly, I laughed. Not from mirth but a solemn, noiseless laugh that welled up inside and demanded release. I gazed intently at Valjean as the insurgents stirred into action.

"'How does it feel?' I asked the walking dead men in the room. 'You call yourselves freemen. Trust me. To a man you will share the same fate as I.'

"In saying this, Charles, I included my nemesis. By day's end, we would pass through Hell's open gates together. I dare say, you and your cohorts have had a busy day receiving all the damnation-bound souls. How much safer France and its Godfearing people could rest without these treasonous, self-aggrandizing dreamers. At the same time, my death would endanger the good citizens of Paris as they faced ever greater dangers from the dark underworld. Right on cue, shots rang out.

"'Everyone to their stations!' Enjolras ordered.

"With great tumult, the doomed insurgents rushed, some from the tavern, others up the stairs to meet the advancing army. As they went, I muttered to their sacrificial backsides, 'We shall meet again on the other side! But I in heaven, you in hell.'"

CHAPTER THE THIRTEENTH:
A BITTER ESCAPE

"**M**y dear Javert, forgive me if I take a step backwards—"

"What do you mean?"

"How would you describe your mental state at the moment Enjolras learned your true identity?

"I felt as if I had arrived at the end of my lifelong battle against John Valjean. Followed by a most surprising—to me—sense of relief."

"Begin with what you call your 'battle' with Valjean."

"From my youth, I believed a just God governed the world. Having Valjean assigned as my executioner seemed, in that moment at least, to balance the scales between the hunted and the hunter. Had I lost my life to any other lowlife thug…. This may sound odd to a man of your station and esteem, Charles. Under any other scenario, the scales of justice might appear out of balance. As I previously detailed, for decades our life paths—Valjean's and mine—had interwoven. The two of us shared a common destiny to one day finish our lifelong duel. A single, final showdown. *Mano a mano*, as the Italians say.

"I always expected the outcome to fall on the side of the angels. But given how the final chapter of my life played out, I welcomed the choice of executioner. Even more, I welcomed the shot that would end my life. Divine symmetry, don't you agree?"

"You wanted to die?"

"Surely not! My envisioned destiny, inscribed—I thought—on the divinely composed scroll of my life, promised, 'You shall breathe your final breath amid the din of street battles between the forces of good and evil—God and Satan.' Thus, my situation in that moment seemed fitting enough—even fulfilling. Could my life—my stellar career—end in any other way?"

"Nonetheless, your words ring of deep regret."

"That my life should end so soon? At the pinnacle of my law enforcement prowess and prospects? So close to my taking command of the entire Prefecture of Paris? Yes. I had fantasized not succumbing to death before the streets of our capital—and all of France—had spit out their last remaining lawbreaker. Having lived and labored day and night, risking life itself, to see the day when the sovereign ruler of France would declare our sacred soil Earth's first-ever crime-free land. Only then might I rightly appear before my Divine Judge saying, 'Take me now, Almighty One. I have accomplished the task for which you brought me into the world and guided me each day to fulfill my destiny.'

"As the decades of my life stormed from one to the next, the toll imposed upon body, mind, and spirit… It exhausted me, Charles. I never admitted to anyone the truth I just shared with you. So there you have it. I have revealed to you my inmost secret self."

"Your admission humbles me, Javert. Continue."

"The rebels left me alone with Jean Valjean. Frankly, I doubted he had the balls—forgive my crudity—to do the bloody deed. If he operated under the guise of his alias, Monsieur Madeleine, the odds favored me. I doubted that coldblooded murder fit the false Mayor's resumé. More likely, he would flee the barricade and disappear into the remotest regions of France or even abroad.

"As I admitted earlier, Charles, my alternate and greater fear had my own French comrades—in the smoke and confusion of battle—explode into the taproom killing everyone in sight—thereby ending my life unrecognized amid that worthless pile of miscreants. Recall that the rebels had stolen my identification. Either way, I prepared to meet my Divine Judge who would surely proclaim, in the words of our Savior himself, 'Come, blessed of my Father, enter into the kingdom prepared for you.'"

"St. Matthew's gospel, Chapter twenty-five, Verse thirty-four."

"Imagine now, Charles, my shock and my disappointment. I speak the truth. From behind the post, Valjean untied the knotted rope fastened around the middle of my body. Then he unbound my wrists. What evil torture had he in mind? Or would we square off and fight each other to the death? If so, despite his superior strength, my training and experience in hand-to-hand combat increased by tenfold at least my chances of conquest.

"Instead, Valjean signaled for me to loosen, but not remove, the rope still looped around my neck. This caused me to think he might trade his pistol for silent death by garrote.

"He then wrapped his closed fist in my already ripped blouse, as one might grab a stubborn beast of burden. With my feet still bound, he dragged me out of the wineshop."

"Why did you not fight to free yourself, Javert?"

"My limbs had numbed from squatting for hours bound to that post. Besides, he held a loaded pistol and had given a sign he knew how to shoot. Any resistance on my part could only end badly—for me.

"With the din and smoke of close-range skirmishes raging, Valjean showed remarkable patience. He slowed to allow me to stagger taking short, deliberate steps.

"The insurgents, intent on withstanding an imminent and final charge, paid us no attention, other than Marius Pontmercy. Twisting my head in the direction of the barricade, I caught a glimpse of that traitor observing our exit from a corner of the now porous barrier. The soon-dead coward smiled and nodded his approval.

"In this manner, we crossed the narrow, shadowed area behind the doomed rebel position. A few paces distant, stacked corpses formed a hideous but to me gratifying—beautiful even—pile of useless rebel trash. Among the heap, I spied a particular female body. Garments bloodied. Her breasts bared and open to view. A single hole in the middle of her chest. 'I know that girl.'

"Valjean made no reply. 'Eponine,' I continued, 'daughter of that Thenardier fellow. She and her brother possessed more courage than their slimy coward of a father.' Charles, that scoundrel allowed his children to die in a cursed rebel cause, while he hid and plotted his next heinous criminal scheme.

"With some difficulty, I crossed the low wall at the end of the alley leading to Mondetour Lane. On the other side, we found ourselves alone, facing each other, two archenemies. Behind us, the close-range battle raged No one to witness Valjean's crime… or my last breath. Fitting, no?

"Valjean thrust the pistol under his arm and fixed on me a look requiring no words to interpret. 'Javert, you know who I am.'

"'I do indeed, 2-4-6-0-1.' I spat each digit at him. 'Beneath whatever alias and disguise you bear in this moment or will in the next, I see only a galley slave. The one France's inadequate laws forced me to parole. Congratulations, then. This dark alley… so typical of your shadowy existence and style. Take your revenge. I welcome it as a martyr for the glory of the people and rightful government of France. May it live on in peace.'

"Valjean drew from his pocket a knife and opened it. 'Aha, a clasp-knife! That suits your kind better, does it not? Why waste a good bullet?'

"Instead, he cut the remaining ropes from about my neck and feet. The look on his face pierced my soul. 'Javert,' he said, 'I have no desire to kill you. Leave this place at once. Begone!'

"Surely I misunderstood. 'What did you say?'

"'I give you your life, as a good cleric once did for me.' A reference to you, Charles."

"Yes. Thank you."

"Then Valjean's voice grew cold. 'Go now! If you look back, I might change my mind.' It takes a great deal to astonish me. Still, I could not repress my shock, my utter… what shall I say? Confusion. Dare I also add, my disappointment? Whatever my tangled web of emotions, I remained motionless.

"Valjean continued, 'I do not expect to emerge from the barricade alive. If, by the grace of God, I do, I want you to know this—'

"'This… what?'

"'Where to find me.'

"Charles, I swear on the Holy Bible I refused to believe what I heard. Had I died and entered another state of existence? He spoke again. 'I currently live under the surname Fauchelevent.'

"'Another alias! How clever. How many does that make?'

"'Listen to me, Javert!' Valjean spoke in soft, measured tones. 'Should I, by some miracle, survive the apocalypse to come, you will find me at home. I live at Rue de l'Homme Arme, Number 7.'

"Suppressing my shock, I repeated, 'Fauchelevent... Rue de l'Homme Arme.'

"'Yes, Number 7. Do not forget. Off with you, Javert. Now!'

"'Number 7,' I repeated, engraving the number on my memory. Safely distant, I turned and spat out my hatred to his vanishing backside, 'You disgust me, Jean Valjean! Far worse, sir, you have... destroyed me!'

"A moment later, as I reached the nearby corner of Rue des Precheurs, a single pistol shot exploded like a cannon behind me. The sound echoed down the street before coming to rest deep within my being. My heart leapt within my chest. In relief? Disappointment? I knew not. Had my nemesis taken his own life? Or— Or worse, had he faked my execution? I preferred the former, but it did not fit the man I knew.

"I pictured him returning to the scene of combat to die in the bloodied street with his rebel comrades, victim of a fatal shot to the heart. I considered Valjean's death the solitary virtuous act he performed for the good of humanity. I turned and spat in his direction, 'Good riddance, 24601!'

"My only regret, Charles? That I did not have the pleasure of pulling the trigger myself. At the same time, I could not shake the chilling sensation of Jean Valjean forever following me with his dead eyes. Once clear of danger, I felt the venom surge from the pit of my stomach. And retched."

"And your next move, Javert?"

"I gathered my wits and returned to headquarters, where I spoke to no one. I rid myself of the disguise I wore in gaining entrance to the rebels' makeshift fortress. I bathed and quickly dressed again in my uniform, donning and buttoning my coat. That done, I stood erect, resuming the customary military stiffness between my shoulders."

CHAPTER THE FOURTEENTH:
THE MAN "SPUN"

"Charles, allow me to explain something about my life's work?"

"By all means, Javert. I possess not a sliver of understanding regarding your career in law enforcement."

"Career? I prefer… sacred vocation."

"As you will. Your state of mind following your narrow escape interests me. That and the events resulting in your subsequent arrival in Afterlife."

"I weary from the telling. More so from this delay regarding my final judgment and departure."

"You claim eagerness to march into the never-ending fires. You seem, even—How shall I put it, Javert?"

"Let me speak more precisely, Charles. From childhood to the day of my… death. I strove to earn my way into a blissful eternity. I dreamed of striding into heaven to the chants of angelic hosts sent to welcome me at heaven's gate. 'Hosanna' they would sing while waving palm branches, as the citizens of Jerusalem did when Jesus entered through the city gates for the last time. Do palm trees exist here in what you call Afterlife? I observe none thus far. Nothing at all, in fact. Only the two of us."

"You shall discover for yourself the answer about trees and other life forms. No two of us experience Afterlife in precisely the same manner."

"To think I almost made it to my last breath 'full of grace'! How could I betray the God of Justice with my last living decision? That, after an exemplary life of self-discipline and spiritual rectitude. How

did I fall into the hands of Satan with my final gasp? But I did. So—
There you have it, Charles. I blame my fall on that demon-in-flesh,
Jean Valjean. Because of him, I stand ready to enter Hell and live out
my sentence of eternal damnation. In truth, I eagerly await its
commencement. I always favored swift justice, either prison or the
guillotine. Thus my impatience with this—what did you call it?"

"Life review."

"If I stood in the place of God judging me—"

"Alas, Javert, neither of us can make that claim. So, let us pick up
where we left off. The events and decisions of that fateful night
interest me."

* * *

"As I said, I blame that cursed Valjean for my final decision!"

"Yet, you—and only you—made every choice governing your
behavior that night. You and no one else scripted the drama that
played out to the end. I urge you, son, own your every deliberate
thought and action."

"I do. But it rends my soul that he initiated the destruction of my
best-laid life plan."

"Javert, I stand ready and eager to guide you through your dark
abyss. I had a reputation on Earth as a good listener. It serves me
well in my present state. We had an expression familiar to you, I'm
sure, 'Time is of the essence.' I assure you, no such rule applies in
Afterlife. On Earth we served the clock, filling our days with
scheduled duties, appointments, and events. In doing so, we forfeited
tyrannical power to time. You have now arrived where time no
longer exists."

"I see no marching band to play my funeral dirge. Where the
medals I earned in the combat of policing the streets of France? I
assure you, Charles, the answer lies in the tragic story about to
unfold. A galling and shameful tale. Before I proceed, let me clarify
for you the central place of my chosen vocation."

"By all means, Javert."

"You know the expression, 'Justice will out'?"

"I do indeed. And believe it so. St. Paul wrote in his letter to the Christians in Rome that, in the mysterious plan of God for each of us and the whole Universe, all that we experience works together for good."

"If you say so. The police and civil courts serve the noble cause of Justice in society. Applied to law enforcement in its day-to-day practice, this demands imperturbable patience, a keen memory for names and places, sounds and faces. A revolt against lawful authority never allows excuse. I can demonstrate from my storehouse of experience every variety of sad tale criminals present as mitigating circumstances in the commission of their heinous crimes, even murder. As if our God in heaven gave them permission to break the law.

"The sovereign laws of the Republic allow no room for malefactors to write their own rules. Rampant chaos would surely paint the sky black in the demise of orderly humanity. Lawlessness run amuck! Should neglect of safety and order threaten to prevail in society—I mean civilized society—only the strictest enforcement of law can safeguard good order and provide assurance of civility and stability. The fate of any society depends on strict enforcement. Without it, what do we have left? Only the irreversible collapse of a proud and once well-ordered nation.

"I swore an oath to uphold the rule of law and execute my duty impeccably. I did just that through four decades of long days and lonely nights until... until. ...A pox on Valjean! He deserved to die from a well-aimed army bullet or from a sword ripping his black heart to shreds. May he rot in Hell! But without our ever crossing paths. Pardon my crude language, Charles."

"I will let the Risen Christ, the final Judge of human hearts, speak for himself at the end of your self-reflection."

"Self-condemnation, you mean."

*   *   *

"Now, Javert, share with me the events of that final, fateful night."

"Must I?"

"Like every man, woman and child who preceded you."

"Including you, Bishop Charles?"

"Including me, a man of many flaws and so many missed opportunities to do still more for my Lord and Savior and the people I served. Begin with what you related earlier. Within an hour of your new freedom, you returned to the Prefecture."

"Correct. Without a backward glance, I resumed my role of police spy, a skill at which I excelled without peer in all of France."

"Forgive the interruption, Javert, but the word, 'spy.' You used it before. May I ask what that entailed?"

"Let me offer a recent example.

"One month prior to the fall of the barricade, I concealed myself along the bank of the Seine nearest to Notre Dame Cathedral. For my hiding place, I chose a slope on the quay. Just beyond the newly repaired Pont des Invalides, lies a favorite escape route for criminals on the run. An iron-grilled gate opens into the Paris sewer system. A portion of the city's effluence flows out from it. Derelicts favor it as a hiding place. God knows why! Most likely because that disgusting system offers safe passage for those willing to risk their lives wading through every form of human filth, including vomit, raw feces, and animal carcasses, at times even a drowned man, woman, or child. The most dedicated policemen—no self-respecting citizen—dares to plunge into that satanic abyss.

"On the night in question, with the black river flowing silently below, I spotted a suspicious-looking man. Of a sudden, he sensed my presence and began to slink away, so I set myself to overtaking him.

"I compare my role as a spy to playing the ravenous feline in a real-life cat-and-mouse game. The keys to my success? A safe, protected distance and utter silence. Better still a moonless night to provide the ideal environment. In this case, neither the cat nor the mouse hurried. I advanced one deliberate step at a time, never allowing him to escape my sight. The goal? Maneuver him into a dead end outside the sewer gate.

"One observing this performance might rightly conclude that the spy setting a trap has a ravenous appetite but without appearing to. It demands craftiness and utmost concentration, not a single overt gesture lest he alarm the mouse.

"To my surprise, the subject of my tracking continued his advance along the quay, falling with every step deeper into my trap. I wondered at his end game. Throw himself into the Seine rather than fall into my hands? To do so meant death at the whims of deadly whirlpools common in that area.

"Following protocols governing arrests in the open streets, I maneuvered him to a spot that allowed no possible escape. We call this strategic maneuver 'spinning' a suspect. The opposite of charging in to make an immediate arrest and risking the prey's escape or bodily harm to oneself. Earlier, anticipating success, I had hired a hackney to stand by out of sight on the dark street above the quay.

"A few feet from where the hunted one planted himself, the effluent's hellish contents discharged through an arched iron grating into the river. Behind the rusty iron bars lay a pitch-dark, vaulted corridor. No sound emanated from anywhere within. Nonetheless, I allowed for the possibility that a partner in crime hid on the other side. My prey folded his arms and stared at the gate with an air of expectation. He tried thrusting it aside. Nothing. He shook it. To no avail. I knew, though he appeared not to, opening his pathway to escape required a key."

"Do I bore you, Charles? I may have told you more than you wished."

"Neither you nor I determine what and how much you share. Full disclosure presents the only path to terminate your life review."

"I welcome Hell's eternal flames! Though unquenchable, they cannot pain me more than reliving my life from this vantage point forward."

CHAPTER THE FIFTEENTH:
JAVERT DECLARES MARIUS DEAD

"Javert, my past experience of guiding souls into eternity prepares me to expect surprises. You may think I know every detail of your life. I do not. I serve only as welcomer and guide, not your biographer. Nor do I stand as your judge. Your angel guardian knows you better than anyone, save our Loving Father, his Son the Christ, and their Holy Spirit. In essence, whether saint or sinner, we examine ourselves, acting as our own witness and jury. But only the Christ who died for us presides as our final judge."

"Charles, I find no suspense in the process laid out before me. With confidence I declare my guilt and now consign myself to Hell. Or a judge to pronounce my sentence. What need have I for further review? I accept the inevitable. So, let us finish this here and now. Make way for me to pass through those wide-open gates."

"Thank you, Javert, for your candid self-assessment. By all means, let us make haste. Onward to the finish line, then. Tell me about your final encounter with Jean Valjean."

"You know about that?"

"It takes not a clairvoyant to surmise that the path of your common destinies had to reach a final dramatic encounter. How else could your story end?"

* * *

"What happened next came as a shock, Charles. At the same time, with great rejoicing. Miracle of miracles, both Valjean and Pontmercy fell into my waiting grasp—a true affirmation of divine benevolence.

In my entire life, I had not experienced such elation, felt so vindicated and rewarded by our Just God. My Creator had chosen me to seize them both and consign the pair to prison for the rest of their lives—at Toulon Prison. Valjean had intimate familiarity with that hellhole, having served there in chains for a majority of his nineteen years."

"My dear Javert, forgive another interruption."

"What now?"

"Jean Valjean shared that heartbreaking story sitting at table alongside my sister, Baptistine, and our dedicated housekeeper, Madame Magloire. How could a sentence so severe fall upon one guilty of such a minor offense as stealing a single loaf to feed his starving sister and her children?"

"Minor offense? Not so, I assure you. Put yourself, if you can, in the shoes of the hardworking tradesman. In addition to suffering the loss of a loaf of bread, the proprietor not only bore the expense of replacing a smashed storefront window but suffered a temporary loss of business. Minor, perhaps to a man of the cloth, accustomed to shriving sinners' heinous violations of moral and civil codes. And even that... sight unseen, separated by the required confessional veil. Add to that his multiple subsequent attempts to escape. I consider two decades in chains far too little to pay for that renegade's unrepented crimes against the State and its law-abiding citizens.

"I cannot expect a man of the cloth to understand that I live—or used to—in the real world of laws and statutes, crime and punishment. In that arena, even our good God expects total compliance, accountability, justice... not profligacy. Nor lenience. No other sentence could fulfill the demands of Justice. I shall say it again, lax enforcement of law sounds the death nell of civilized society. I grant that God cleanses a soul through sincere repentance. The flesh, however, must pay society's price for even the most minor malfeasance.

"Did there not exist an alternative to punishment, Javert?"

"Let me tell you about your mythical alternative, Charles. Rampant chaos will run amuck in that benighted, misbegotten land. I swear this on my official papers of assignment as angel guardian of all good, honest, right-living people within France and her colonies.

"I expect the same standard to apply in the application of Divine Justice now, in what you call Afterlife. I seek no mercy, no quarter for the unforgivable sin of ending my own life. Any alternate outcome represents an offense against divine order on earth and, I dare say, in this my strange new state of being. Absolute and unconditional forgiveness can only classify as weakness on the part of our all-powerful God. To believe anything other? Impossible, Charles. Certainly, you agree."

"On that point, Javert, we have reached an impasse."

"We have, except… my knowledge of divinely ordained justice trumps that of a prelate of the Church. Monseigneur, your misguided naivete… well, it shocks me."

"Javert, we must wait… see… and, as you say, obey our Divine Judge. For now, let us move on."

"If no alternative exists."

*   *   *

"Charles, the events I relate to you now happened the same night the barricade fell. As described earlier, at the prefecture I changed from my disguise into the full accoutrement of my office. Let me remind you of my rank as second in command to the Paris Prefect. Some defenders of law and order take pride in their death count in the performance of their duty. For my part, I consider death a favor to the criminal. It results when called for but only as a last resort. Best to let a wrongdoer ponder his sins in a dank cell cohabited by the filthiest human scum crawling the face of this earth or, preferably, in a ship's stifling, hope-crushing galley.

"On the unlikely chance that a gaggle of rebels had escaped the barricade or run from battle to seek refuge within the bowels of Paris, I chose a vantage point not far from the same locked gate I described for you earlier. This position offered the cover of concealing shadows not more than a few quick steps away. Whoever might hide behind that polluted opening had no chance of detecting my presence. On that same June night, sufficient moonlight reflected off the river to offer the additional advantage of exposing the spot of departure.

"For more than an hour, I kept vigil in alert expectation. Should I return to the prefecture? Experience had taught me to stay the course even until dawn, if necessary. An hour later, I sensed activity inside the locked grate. My veteran's judgment demanded a state of utmost alert.

"In the next silent moment, I spied shadowy, unrecognizable human forms moving behind the grate. Not a minute passed before it swung open! Someone inside, other than my prey, possessed a key. Undoubtedly a pickpocket had purloined it from an unwitting sewage-flow monitor. The door edged open with the shrill shriek of long-rusted joints. It sounded much the same as an old man rising from bed to a cacophony of creaking, crackling bones.

"Unknown to the underworld scum, I poised myself ready to spring from my hiding place and make swift arrests. Should I discover more than two rats, I would signal my waiting hackney driver to fetch backup officers from the nearby prefecture.

"Two male figures emerged. One carried the other fellow who apparently sustained an injury too severe to allow wading on his own through the gagging muck. Could it be? Only one man in all my police experience had the strength and endurance to carry another through putrid sewage all the way to the riverbank.

"'Praise the choirs of angels and all the holy saints in heaven,' I whispered when I identified the clear and unmistakable form of my nemesis Jean Valjean. My lifelong thorn had stepped unwittingly into my waiting trap. Having somehow escaped death amid the slaughter at the barricade, the pair now sought improbable freedom. Or had they run away in terror of imminent defeat? Such a conclusion did not fit the Valjean I knew. This gratuitous blessing affirmed my faith. 'Yes!' I breathed, 'a just God rules our universe.'"

*   *   *

"The stink of raw sewage reached my hiding place as soon as the beast and his lowlife burden quit the sewer. I covered my nose with my sleeve to keep from gagging. Valjean locked the grate and returned the key to his shadowed partner inside.

"Imagine my glee if you can, Charles. As a man of the holy cloth, you may have no concept of what I felt in that instant. Earlier, Valjean gave back my life. Now I held his in my righteous grasp. Do you think I owed him some measure of reciprocal mercy for saving my life? In your world perhaps. Not in mine. Never!

"Valjean laid his comrade-in-treason on the quay. The younger fellow showed no control of his limbs. Not so much as a twitch when deposited on the bank. If Valjean's burden had survived the barricade, he died in the sewer, a fitting burial site for a filthy revolutionary."

"Clearly, you relished the moment, Javert."

"I did, Charles. I did. The scene played out apparition-like on this stage of veiled moonlight and shadow. I expected Valjean to roll the body into the river in hope of escaping unencumbered into the balmy Paris night. When he didn't, I chose that moment to step into the open. Glancing my way, our eyes met. Valjean's gaze registered instant recognition… but not fear.

"We each had visions but quite different, I assure you. He became aware that he had fallen from one danger into a level of peril more distasteful even than the sewer. Would you believe, Charles? Valjean's feces-smeared face emitted. …How might I describe it? Dare I call it angelic glow? Perhaps better the smile of a man grateful for his first breath of fresh air. For my part, I found no mirth in the situation, whether angelic or diabolical. My return gaze projected mastery, followed by disgust then delated vindication after a lifetime of losses.

"Making sure he took note of the bludgeon in my fist, I spoke in a curt, calm voice, 'Your name?' I wanted him—needed him—to say it aloud, to admit, at last, I had won our decades-long, seesaw battle.

"'You already know,' came the answer.

"'I demand a name.'

"'Jean Valjean. You now have me in your power, Inspector Javert.'

"Of a sudden, my sense of utter and complete triumph overcame my desire to control my emotions and remain erect. I clamped my bludgeon between my teeth, bit down and bent my knees, inclining my upper body forward. Forcing my will to regain mastery over this undesired reflex, I straightened myself.

"Ignoring his disgusting piss and shit-covered body, I clamped one vicelike hand on Valjean's unresisting shoulder. The other held my cudgel at the ready. Our faces almost touched. Like a zebra foal submitting to the overpowering tusks of a mastodon, Valjean remained inert beneath my grasp. He appeared to have expended the last of his formidable strength getting himself and his burden through the maze and out of the sewer.

"'Jean Valjean, again I possess your miserable being. After all these years and now for the rest of your thieving, lying life, I have the pleasure of placing you under arrest. I have longed for this moment since the day I handed you that parole document. Against my better judgment. Some incompetent judge's order mandated your release. Henceforth, Valjean, I shall see you consigned to the galleys where you belonged during these many years you stole from your country.' His reply puzzled me.

"'Inspector, I stand ready. Do with me what you will.'

"Charles, could I trust a wily escape artist like Valjean? That chameleon of many aliases and disguises? No, but I chose to play along with his little game. 'Prisoner 24601, you shall soon wish our all-just God had allowed you to die alongside your fellow insurrectionists.'

"'Inspector,' his tone flat, even disengaged, 'I have regarded myself your prisoner since this morning. As proof of my intent, I offered you my address, both street and number. I have no intention of escaping. Take me now. I yield to you as your prisoner.'

"'My prisoner indeed, Valjean. At last. Identify your fallen comrade here.'

"'Marius. Marius Pontmercy.'

"'Hah! I know him. A self-aggrandizing lawyer! God favored him with an early death.'

"'Javert,' Valjean said, 'I beg only one favor.'"

*   *   *

"Charles, in my state of ecstasy and vindication, I admit to barely hearing what my prisoner had just uttered. I stood on the brink of closing my thick, detailed portfolio in which I had chronicled his felonious post-parole life. It began with the theft of forty sous from that helpless chimneysweep. I remember the boy's name even. Gervais. And this, not more than a few days following his too-generous parole from the galleys. His first seemingly modest crime vindicated my judgment that, in Jean Valjean I possessed conclusive proof of my theory: once a law-breaker, a man possesses always and forever the indelible taint of criminal blood.

"Now, after a lifetime of miscreant behavior and ill-intent, prisoner 24601 would rot in confinement. At least, until God in heaven saw fit to summon him to pass through the gates of Hell into eternal damnation. How could I foresee that but a few hours later fate would have me standing here with you on the doorstep of my own personal and eternal Hell?"

"Javert, I find your certitude about your eternal fate… impressive. But again I remind you, your tragic story has not yet reached its conclusion."

"'Thankfully, Charles, we approach the end of my tragic tale. In response to Valjean's insane request, I responded, 'You dare to ask a favor? I know your wiles. Take the boy home? Bah!'

"Keeping my eyes riveted on Valjean, I thrust my lips upwards toward his nose in a scowl of savage revelry. 'You surrendered your right to ask anything, let alone a favor, as you call it. I shall count this foolish lad as your final victim.'

"Valjean replied, 'Javert, I speak regarding this boy lying at your feet. Dispose of me as you see fit. But first, I ask one kindness from you. Help me to deliver him home to his aged grandfather.'

"'Do you still regard me fool enough to grant you, of all people, the slightest concession?' Do you know, Charles, what came as a shock to me?"

"I cannot unless you tell me."

"I did not reject his outrageous request the instant it reached my ears. My typical response in similar situations? 'This man does not concern me. Toss him in the river for all I care. I place you under arrest and on your way to prison for the rest of your useless life.'

"Valjean bent over, drew from his pocket a damp, soiled handkerchief. He wiped Marius's blood-stained brow. 'As you see, I brought him from the barricade through the sewers.'"

"'No, 24601! He died in the sewer.'"

"Valjean barked, 'Not dead! Not yet.' After which he went silent, seeming to gather his thoughts. 'He lives with his grandfather, a nobleman, in the district of Marais. The goodman's name I do not know.'

"Valjean then fumbled in Marius's coat again and produced a damp and soiled pocketbook. He opened it to a page on which the young man had penciled something. He held the water-blurred page before me. The barely sufficient light in that spot allowed me to decipher but a few lines. 'Gillenormand, Rue des Filles-du Calvaire, No. 6.' A nobleman, you say?'

"'Yes.'

"With a deep sigh, I signaled to my coachman. A moment later, the carriage descended the incline to the quay."

*   *   *

"With admirable tenderness, Valjean laid the boy on the rear bench. He then sat alongside me facing the deceased rebel. The smell of them fouled the interior and soiled the upholstery. I wondered how much the driver might demand in recompense. I slammed the carriage door shut, and we ascended the quay. Once at street level, the coachman whipped up his rested horses. We made haste through the city's empty streets in the direction of the Bastille.

"A silence of the dead reigned within the carriage as the cabbie made his way to Rue des Filles-du Calvaire. Marius's body lay motionless. His head drooped to his breast; his right arm dangled to the floor. Next for him, a coffin."

CHAPTER THE SIXTEENTH:
A FALL FROM GRACE

"**S**hare with me, if you will, Javert, your state of mind as you approached the Pontmercy residence?"

"Must I resurrect that moment, too, Charles?"

"In Afterlife, 'must' does not exist. Only 'need to.'"

"I can refuse to answer?"

"Yes. However—"

"'What?'

"You will find it impossible. Our loving Father supplies us with words and resurrects long-forgotten memories."

"Speak not to me of fathers, loving or otherwise! I told you about the rat who sired my entry into that ugly, crime-infested world."

"Javert, the need for disclosure rises up from within you. It comes upon you as an inner craving, denying the possibility of restraining your desire to withhold the truth. Whether the words flow easily or with great affliction to your soul—trust me—they will come. They will."

"Charles, I find myself in hazardous territory. I fear my ability to survive what comes next."

"Survive? My son, you left physical life and death behind. Only eternal life stretches ahead of you."

"You ask me to play the role of explorer, like Jacques Cartier charting the New World's wild, uncharted western rivers and lush landscapes. I bear no resemblance to that man, Charles. I functioned best where I knew the rules in advance and followed France's divinely inspired legal code. To the letter."

"I do understand the difficulty you face, my dear Javert. In Afterlife, each soul arrives as an open book in the presence of our God. Here there exist no masks, no disguises, no half-truths behind which to conceal our past or predict the future. We present ourselves to our Creator with our triumphs and failures laid bare. I confess from my own experience the truth of what I now share with you. Like you, I desired to mask my mistakes and give light only to my short list of virtues. Fight this truth as we will, we cannot avoid revealing the full-length drama we call our life, with no jot or tittle unrevealed. This requires laying your Earth life bare, all things revealed and fully owned."

"With due respect, Charles, the outcome of my story contains no mystery. Like a good policeman in the employ of heaven, you must obey your charge to usher me to the gates of Hell. There we part. For all eternity. You shall never see me or hear my voice again, no matter the volume of my involuntary cries of suffering in that perpetual furnace."

"For now, Javert, your story lacks only an ending scene. When ready, please go on."

"Having no portal of escape, I shall reveal the horror of what happened on the street outside the home of Pontmercy... and after."

*　　　　*　　　　*

"At every jolt over the stony pavement, a drop of blood trickled from the young rebel's hair. Confusion engulfed me. I equated this evidence with the possibility of some waning inner lifeforce struggling to return from the dead.

"When my carriage arrived at the entrance to Rue des Filles-du-Calvaire, I alighted first to verify the number on the carriage gate. Satisfied, I strode to the entrance door and raised the heavy iron knocker. In doing so, I made out the image of a satyr fixed in an attitude of hostile confrontation. I sent the knocker swinging hard and inward toward the door plate. Upon striking the receiving piece, a violent peal echoed up and down the empty street. In truth, I wanted to awaken the residents asleep in every home along that tranquil lane. They needed to see the return of the dead insurrectionist as an object lesson of the power of the French Army and police. When not a single newly lit candle brightened any neighboring window, this indifference only added to my annoyance.

"Charles, when law-abiding citizens in the better parts of a city get a whiff of revolt, or should some other public turmoil erupt, they take refuge in slumber, like children fearing the Bugaboo's coming. They dull their hearing beneath warm and heavy coverlets, as if burrowing their heads into a pile of sand.

"The porter appeared at the door in nightclothes. A single candle shook in his right hand. He struggled to keep an open eye. 'Who're you?' he managed in a gravelly, deep-of-night growl. 'Everyone in the house has retired. Come back at a decent hour in the morning.' Recognizing my uniform, the old man came to attention. 'I beg your pardon, officer. Who do you seek?'

"The foul-odored Jean Valjean, with minimal aid from our visibly upset coachman, removed Pontmercy from the carriage. Valjean supported the boy's dead weight like a mother who comforts a sick and frightened child. A scene I never once experienced. What did I know, therefore, about a mother's comfort?

"I kept a close eye on him. No more wily suspect existed in all of France. I learned from having lost him too many times in the past— to my personal shame and discredit.

"I addressed the porter in a tone befitting a government official. 'I seek a gentleman, a nobleman, known by the surname Gillenormand.'

"'What do you want with him?' the porter dared to ask.

"In any other instance, I would arrest such a man on the grounds of unwillingness to provide factual information to an officer of the law. 'Tell him I have brought his grandson back.'

"'His… grandson?'

"'You dolt! Look at him. Surely dead. Victim of a revolt perpetrated by a band of traitorous schoolboys. This lad among them. All died in battle.' I glanced behind me at Valjean, tattered and smelling every bit like a giant turd. 'Except this lout here. And I shall soon deliver him to prison. After a good hosing down.'

"The porter surveyed the boy's body with an expression of horror.

I informed him, 'This misbegotten lad fought at the doomed barricade. He died there from his wounds. You'll need to prepare him for burial. Go at once! Wake his grandfather. You and all who dwell within will surely have a funeral here tomorrow.'

"The coachman struggled with the lad's feet, keeping them from dragging on the ground. Careful at the same time not to let a drop of the dead rebel's blood soil his clothing and the residence's thick carpeting. In this manner, they bore the corpse past the unbelieving porter and into the residence. The porter remained a frozen ice sculpture. 'Go, man! I must hurry to get this man to the prefecture.'

"He nodded stupidly and rushed up the staircase—as best he could—to awaken someone, the housekeeper most likely. Soon enough, an old woman appeared at the top of the stairs. Without identifying himself, Valjean carried the young man's body up the stairs and deposited it on a settee in the hallway.

"I motioned to Jean Valjean. He understood and hastily descended, as promised. I put not the slightest trust in his feigned submissiveness. I followed him cudgel in hand to the waiting carriage. We took our seats while the coachman took his time mounting his box before signaling his horse to move.

"'Inspector Javert.' Valjean spoke in a calm and even gentle voice, 'I beg you, grant me yet one more favor.'

"What kind of fool did this brazen criminal think me that I could not foresee another of his wizardly escape plans? I pretended not to hear him.

"'Inspector,' he said again. This time louder.

"'What?' I demanded.

"'Allow me to go home… for just a moment. Then, you shall do whatever you like with me. I swear to you… I shall not resist.'

"I remained silent, my chin withdrawn deep into the collar of my coat. Then… then I lowered the glass and spoke these hitherto unimaginable words. 'Driver, Rue de l'Homme Arme. No. 7.' How appropriate, Charles. Armed Man Street."

CHAPTER THE SEVENTEENTH:
COMMOTION IN THE ABSOLUTE

"You acted rightly, Javert, allowing Valjean to bid farewell to his adopted daughter."

"Rightly, Charles? Perhaps in your ecclesial world. Not in mine. I never made such a concession in all the decades of my unblemished career. Never once!"

"In your mind, then, this act of kindness had SIN stamped on it?"

"A far too lenient label. I consider it the worst form of betrayal. On a par with treason against the state. Worthy of execution by the guillotine. 'Damnation' better captures the situation."

"Betrayal? Treason? Damnation? Such extreme labels."

"Yes, treason against my sworn allegiance to the laws of our sacred land. And therefore against God."

"How sad, Javert. I eagerly await reliving with you the next scene in this melodrama. Proceed, my friend."

*   *   *

"You already know the worst of my sins. Even Hell with its deep cauldron of eternal flames might reject my unworthy soul."

"You forget, Javert, I do not drive this coach. That task falls to you alone."

"Alone… yes. Neither Valjean nor I spoke during the ride to Rue de l'Homme Arme in the badly soiled carriage. Over and over, I commanded myself to cry out to the driver, 'Stop this instant!' And to myself, 'Javert, put your prey in jail or risk sinking deeper into your self-dug hellhole.' My muddled brain sought to piece together whatever escape plan my captive had concocted. Could it prove so simple as to bid a final farewell to Fantine's bastard daughter? Once secure in the prefecture, Valjean would never know freedom again.

"In a parallel scenario, I nursed the nagging feeling this wizard of disguise had concocted some arcane plan to escape before we reached the station. But who would grant refuge to a man who had bathed in the Paris sewer while carrying a dead man on his back?

"I swore to the God of Justice to make Valjean pay dearly for the countless stolen days he owed the honest, law-abiding citizens of France.

"But… why this sudden charade of docility? Why had the man of overpowering strength and resilience not resisted… yet? Had he, in Jesus' words, used his ill-gotten money to make friends for himself, so they might offer welcome and hide him in their homes?

"I allowed myself not a gram of trust in Prisoner 24601's words and promises. I vowed to martial my keenest physical and mental skills to counter whatever mode of escape he plotted. The only sound as we made our way in the silence and blackness of the night? The clip-clop of the horse's hooves on the cobblestone and the clucking of the driver's tongue, as he guided the stubborn beast through near lightless streets. I swore a vow as pure and holy as any cloistered monk's not to let him out of my sight.

"Charles, I need to backtrack."

"Very well."

"I hoped never to reveal the sickening memory of a night years ago in Thenardier's Paris tenement lodging."

"It all comes out, Javert. You cannot to keep any relevant part of your life hidden."

"Do you recall my telling you about the night I cornered Thenardier and his partners in crime?"

"I do."

"Well, I also had Valjean within my grasp in that closed-in tenement apartment. Only to let him slip away. Again. I let the exuberance of my successful coup in rounding up that weasel's gang of thugs distract me from another, silent presence in the shabby residence. I hadn't paid sufficient attention to their prisoner—Let me restate that. I made the ill-fated assumption that, in the former innkeeper and his gang of thugs, I already had my prize.

"I compounded my dereliction of duty by not identifying the seemingly unwitting citizen at the window. In doing so, I violated a prime principle of policing—never assume. During my arrest of the crooks, Jean Valjean, the biggest prize of all, escaped unnoticed out the second story window.

"I swear to you, Charles, I had never made such a blunder in all my decorated career. And I never did again. I learned my lesson the hard way... but I did learn."

"I believe you, Javert."

"In erring, I let down the Law to which I had dedicated my life and intended to serve faithfully to my last breath. Never again, Charles. I dread this distasteful, embarrassing confession. Must I act as my own flawed advocate before a jury of angels and my Divine Judge? I tarnished my vocation, my very *raisson d'etre*. You agree to that much, do you not?'"

"You need neither my opinion nor my affirmation, Javert. Again I urge you not to render hasty judgment on yourself. See this process to the end. I possess no power to condemn you and will not violate the objectivity of my mission. Like everyone before you, you shall learn your fate... but only when this review reaches its conclusion. And I beg you not to regard me as anything other than your nonjudgmental guide through the maze of your life."

"Which shall conclude when?"

"When you have reviewed your tale's final scene."

"So, let us proceed then, Charles! Like two soldiers marching into a war's deciding battle, eh?"

"An apt image. One unheard in any previous companioning assignment."

*　　　　*　　　　*

"Valjean had petitioned me to stop at his home on the way to the prefecture. My only desire? To see my lifelong nemesis removed from Godfearing society for the rest of his days. So, why had I directed the driver to change course? Will I ever find an answer to that question, Charles?"

"Indeed you will, Javert. I promise you that."

*   *   *

"On that fateful carriage ride to Rue de l'Homme Arme, I sat face to face with Valjean. Twenty times at least on the way to his residence a strident voice cried out within me. That hated man enraged and inspired me in the same instant. I nursed a desire to fling myself upon Valjean, seize him, put him in irons, bury him once and for all time in France's most secure prison.

"All I had to do—deliver him to my station with the gloating words of a conquering hero, 'I have in my clutches a fugitive from justice and the only survivor of this day's failed rebellion. Honorable Prefect, I deliver him into your hands. May he never again see daylight in what remains of his wretched life.' Thence to leave Javert in the hands of the prison system and rid myself of the matter forever. The epitome of justice served."

"Still, Javert, you refrained from acting on your conviction."

CHAPTER THE EIGHTEENTH:
JAVERT OFF THE TRACK

"At the entrance to Rue de l'Homme Arme, I ordered the carriage to halt. The location of Valjean's home offered him the advantage of familiarity with the surrounding neighborhood. Observing the street's narrow entrance, I judged it impossible for our carriage to enter. Seeing my disadvantage, I ratcheted my professional instincts to a state of utmost alert.

"Exiting our transport in the dark of night placed me in a vulnerable predicament. To reach his home meant walking, I reckoned, thirty meters to the front entrance. The darkness of that path heightened my peril.

"On that dark night, I had little chance of corralling Valjean should he bolt and run off into his well-charted environs. My option in that scenario? Roust and jail everyone in his household as accessories. Including Fantine's daughter should I find her inside. The charge? Aiding and abetting—harboring a wanted criminal.

"As yet, I told myself, Valjean had given me no reason to suspect he intended to do more than bid farewell. Or that he had preplanned an escape. Before I alighted from the carriage, the coachman interrupted me.

"'*Monsieur l'Inspecteur*, I beg your indulgence but the blood of that dead man soaked the Utrecht velvet I purchased and installed just last week. Not to mention—the assassin's filth.' He punctuated this by pinching his nostrils and adding without a trace of shame, 'I ask a fair indemnity.' He withdrew a notebook from his pocket and had the audacity to add, 'If the Inspector would kindly write an attestation to the effect that I have no blame for this dam—'

"I thrust the notebook aside. 'How much do you want, including your time and the drive?'

"'It comes to seven hours and a quarter. Plus replacement of my new velvet seats. Honorable Inspector, eighty francs should cover my time and the repairs.'

"I withdrew from my pocket four napoleons, each valued, as you know, at twenty francs.

"I alighted from the carriage first, then Valjean stepped down still shackled at the wrists. Upon reaching No. 7, he pounded his fist on the door. Several times. When the door opened, he looked to me for permission.

"'Yes… go upstairs.'

"Had I truly uttered those words? Impossible! But I could not deny it.

"After a long pause during which Valjean studied my odd expression, I spoke as I had never—ever—spoken. It took all my strength to force the words out of my mouth. 'I will wait for you here.' I then, God help me, removed his shackles!

"Valjean studied my eyes in disbelief. I conceded only because I envisioned the outcome. Had he not made up his mind to surrender himself and make an end of his decades-long flight? This cat granted a measure of liberty to his ensnared mouse… but only to the length of my claws.

"Valjean entered the house. I trained my eyes on him as he ascended the stairs until he reached the landing. On arriving there, he paused. A window stood open to allow a mite of ventilation on that breathless night. It also offered a view onto the street and the carriage. I… I then—I cannot go on, Charles. I cannot force the words from my soul."

"Don't stop, Javert. As you have learned, it will come out. I know you understand that."

"'I returned to the entrance of the house and…'"

"Take it slowly, Javert."

"I walked to the gate, paused, and continued out to the street."

"And?"

"Must I say it?"

"Yes."

"I dismissed the coach… and walked to the Prefecture—alone."

*   *   *

"What did you feel in that moment, Javert?"

"How can I describe the avalanche of turmoil pounding within my chest and broiling my brain?"

"Trust me. You will find the words."

"I'd never trusted anyone before, not in my whole life, not since the misbegotten day I first fell from that evil woman's womb. I expect no one to understand the mix of feelings erupting within me. In releasing Valjean and walking away alone, I bore on my conscience the greatest sin of my life. I had violated my sworn oath to uphold the Law… and bring all varieties of criminal scum to justice. To my eternal shame, I felt… for the first time…"

"Name it, Javert. Doing so here before your God and all the holy angels you will find safe haven."

"Release… pure relief… from my lifelong burden, the load I'd carried from one decade to the next. In the next instant, I hated myself. What I had done would condemn me for the rest of my life… to the same prisons I had filled during my previously unscathed record of service to the Law. I fell into a deep pit where blackness filled my being. Would you believe, Charles? I took what I would call… terrifying pleasure in my fall from grace."

"Opposites, Javert, but not uncommon in each one's life. My own experience of such a state? Escape from the Revolution with my bride. In our case the opposites consisted of fear of the unknown and the thrill of starting a new life together… with no one to answer to but ourselves."

"So you know, at least in part, Charles."

"Forgive me for interrupting your narrative."

"I lumbered through a misty drizzle that evolved into on and off showers. As I walked, I morphed by turns into my own advocate, defendant, prosecutor, and jury. In the role of judge, I pronounced the verdict. 'The jury finds you, *former* Inspector Javert, guilty of wanton failure to perform your most solemn duty. Therefore, I consign you to prison at Toulon, where you shall take your place on the galley ships. Case dismissed. I order you to remove this traitor from my court. And, Javert, may God have mercy on your misbegotten soul… if you have one."

*　　　　*　　　　*

"Where did I leave off, Charles?"

"You walked away from Valjean's residence, leaving him to live in peace without your long shadow appearing at every crossroad, before or behind him, to the right or left. You then portrayed your own trial on the charge of grave malfeasance of duty."

"To my shame, I confessed to that crime. In doing so, I experienced the worst hour of my life."

"Such a strong word, shame. Not the label I would attach to these events. To this listener, they appear more like the dawn of an awakening heart."

"Nonsense! With due respect, Charles, I cannot expect a bishop who spent his life in the sacred service of Holy Mother Church to understand a policeman's life or his decisions."

"I assure you, Javert, I heard the words you spoke and correctly interpreted them. Furthermore, I believe every word of the story as you related it. However—"

"What?"

"I deem your decision not as a moral failure, rather as a moment of… intense spiritual growth."

"If I may speak my mind—"

"By all means, Javert."

"I judge you wholly mistaken, sir. I had lived my entire life as you did, faithful before the throne of God to my divine calling, my destined vocation. Until that climactic moment, I'd kept myself unblemished, striving for righteousness and justice in flawless service to our fatherland.

"Had Jean Valjean carried out his assigned duty to put a bullet in my brain, you, Charles, would now escort me directly to the throne of a smiling, grateful, rewarding God. I imagine choirs of winged angels chanting, 'Well done, good and faithful servant, take your rightful place among the saints in the heights of heaven.'

"Instead—and I mean no disrespect, Charles—I find you blocking my way to the Fallen Angel's fiery realm."

"I repeat, Javert, your final destination awaits completion of this examen of your life. I urge you, then, deflect any premature assumptions. You cannot usurp the role of your final, Divine Judge. I ask patient endurance on your part."

"You speak in riddles, Charles. And, I deal only in facts, observable acts. Let us get on with it, then."

"Yes, it appears we have arrived at the final scene of your personal drama."

*   *   *

"So, 'the play's the thing,' Charles. I don't recall where or when I heard this. Or its source. Would that my life had proved nothing more than a stage play with a grand finale and grateful bows to an applauding audience. I might then envision myself resuming my life as a decorated officer of the Paris police. Fantasy of fantasies! Instead, this melodrama grinds on toward a real-life villain's death and eternal damnation."

"Carry on, then."

"After leaving Valjean's residence, an irreversible change took place within me. Not for the better. Anxiety compressed my whole being. On that muggy, showery June night, I trudged past silent residences along Rue de l'Homme Arme on a direct course to the prefecture, or so I thought. Without planning to do so, I veered off course to the banks of the River Seine at the Quai des Ormes.

"For the first time in my professional life, I walked with my chin pressing the top of my rib cage, both hands locked behind my back in a posture I'd witnessed in countless shuffling, silent convicts. Prior to that night, I strode with head high, arms folded across my chest, my cudgel clutched tightly in my fist, and my soul confident of performing God's sacred work. I halted some distance from the Place du Chatelet, at the angle of the Pont Notre Dame. You must know the place, Charles."

"You flood me with memories from my youth, Javert. Pleasant ones. I strolled along that route many times before the revolution detoured my life. Never that late at night, however."

"At that spot, I stopped and leaned both elbows on the parapet, chin resting between my splayed fingers. Mariners dread that stretch of the Seine. No one falling in from that location ever reappeared. Ever. Brash swimmers drown at that spot while showing off their strength and endurance skills."

"What happened on the parapet, Javert."

"The unspeakable. Had I lived beyond that fateful night, I might have…"

"What, my son? What might you have done… or become?"

"Withheld my crimes from my superiors. Revealed nothing regarding the two escaped insurgents, one of them living, the other deceased. I entwined my fingers… fully intending to move on with my life. Can you believe, Charles? I cannot reveal what followed. Pride forbids sharing the words, even in this altered state of being."

"You can do it, Javert. You must."

"I… I contemplated."

"Ahh. Tell me about your… contemplation."

"A novelty, a revolution, a catastrophe had risen to power in the foundation of my being. Never had I felt the need or ever once entertained a desire to engage in reflective inventory of my interior self."

"It stands to reason that this might have caused a bout of unaccustomed spiritual suffering. Grant yourself some inner space, Javert. What may now seem prolonged agony—"

"I know, I know… lasts but a billionth of half a second in Earth time."

"Exactly."

*   *   *

"A ghastly catastrophe shook me to the depths of my being. I had done something unthinkable. My brain, ever sharp, always alert to my surroundings, had succumbed to cognitive blindness. My thought processes lost their accustomed transparency. For several hours, I ceased to be—how shall I put it?"

"Simple?"

"Exactly, Charles. That's the very word. Without warning, thinking cleaved my conscience. Worse, I possessed no power to manage or curtail, let alone silence my internal struggle. I, Inspector Javert, found myself at the mercy of... the words catch in my throat... alternate possibility."

"How terrifying for you. Most people on earth discern opposing paths daily. The need to choose one, reject the other."

"Not Inspector Javert! Never! Having released Valjean, I saw ahead of me two straight but contrary paths. Could Javert entertain opposing options? Never!

"I owed my life to an inveterate malefactor. Do I now honor that debt? Repay it in kind? I reduced myself to the level of that same notorious fugitive from justice. Repay John Valjean with leniency? Say to him, 'Go free, my friend. Thank you for restoring my life?' Impossible! Sacrifice my career to personal gratitude? I preferred death to falling so low.

"In all my life, I had never betrayed society. I remained true to my best principles. The most effective guardians of Law set moral conscience aside at the stationhouse door. Once a recruit dons the uniform, the Law becomes the voice of God. I never entertained the possibility of conflict between duty and personal inclinations. To acknowledge the possibility of a second way, choose one option over the other... the very thought turned my stomach.

"That Jean Valjean had given back my life... that a criminal on the run from the Law had done me a favor, one calling for... reciprocity! I sought to comprehend my position, find again my true north. In vain did I look for an alternative to my bitter-tasting dilemma.

"Deliver Jean Valjean to the magistrates for sentencing, as he deserved? My reformulating conscience refused to allow it. To grant him freedom, however, meant falling from lofty grace to a level lower than a convict. I had perpetrated the worst violation possible for an esteemed servant of the State. The end in either case? Dishonor. Discharge. Death of the life I had lived, loved, and sacrificed body and soul for since childhood."

"Javert, my son, you suffered greatly sorting this dilemma. The turmoil you experienced far outweighs any trials I faced during my lifetime. I can only thank you for opening your interior life to me."

"Your words comfort me, Charles, but they arrive too late to rescue me."

"With every confession you grow in my estimation of your character. Let me remind you, Javert, that I am—"

"Not my final judge."

"Exactly."

"This may sound strange to you, and I would never admit it to anyone but you, Charles. Would you like to know my greatest fear?"

"Only if you need to share it."

"Forcing myself to… think. The violence of conflicting options forced me to allow the possibility of searching for a different solution. Prior to that moment, I yielded my personal decisions to the Law and to my superiors who upheld and administered it."

"What seems a curse to you, Javert, I see as a blessing. So, then, we have not yet reached the final act of your story?"

"Very astute, Charles. Consider that the very act of thinking… weighing the pros and cons of any issue, crept into my soul with the stealth of a midnight burglar. Alternate ways of thinking arrived as sources of pain beyond anything I ever experienced. Surely, you now must agree that I shall never pass through the gates of Paradise. So tell me, saintly soul, what you think of me."

"What do I think, Javert? Hmm. Let me begin by saying the process of contemplation arrives sometimes as an irritating rash on one's body, causing physical stress and discomfort to one's whole being. The result, violent internal rebellion. Philosophers call the product of this struggle *persona*."

"I a philosopher? Never!"

*   *   *

"Prolonged thought on any subject triggers some degree of

fatigue, Javert. And spiritual. In your case, I might call what you experienced unbearable internal torture both in the instant and now in the retelling."

"I know a good deal about physical torture, Charles, though I never suffered it myself. Doubt? Mental suffering? Not in my experience. Ever."

"The key to sound thinking and growth demands—I repeat, *demands*—exploration of one's conscience. The pain of thought heightens in severity as we repress our sensitivity to that voice."

"I value your opinion, Charles. What remedy might I find?"

"The only antidote after suffering such a shock calls for rendering a complete and honest account of oneself. You have done this well in my presence. I urge you not to resist this sacred truth. Free it. Allow it to escape its dank hiding place and thrive in the healing sunshine of truth."

"I fear we do not speak the same language, Charles. May we move on?"

"As you wish."

"At the end of my bout with the powers of darkness and light, I arrived, as you know, at the decision to release Valjean. In doing so, I spat in the face of police regulations. Worse, I acted contrary to the entire social and judicial edifice. Contrary to the hallowed statutes of the Civil Code, I substituted my personal conviction, disregarding the law requiring me to bring that criminal to long overdue justice. The price—? Despite my bravado, I tremble in anticipation of that payment coming due. I surrender myself to our Creator's eternal design for the punishment of traitors such as I."

"Let me assure you, Javert. All the heavenly hosts applaud your decision to free Valjean."

"You mean well, Charles, but I live—lived—in a different world compared to your surrender of self to the Church. In my case, the deluge fought back at me with daunting force. A shrill voice reaching me from some unseen region of the universe scolded me. 'Return in haste to Rue de l'Homme Arme—'"

"Number 7."

"You remember. Instinct commanded me to commit Jean Valjean

to prison without a moment's delay. That voice affirmed my best interests... promised restoration of my reputation... rebirth of my career. All hung in the balance. 'Do your Christian duty!' it growled beastlike, 'No one need know the details and circumstances of your narrow escape from the barricade.'"

"Still, you acted contrary to that nagging voice."

"I did. A voice of equal authority barred my way."

"You even declare God subservient to your Civil Law. True, Javert?"

"Not at all! How could you of all people propose such a false conclusion? God and Law form equal and inseparable forces for good. Two halves of the one whole of life.

"A galley slave sacred? Never! Allow a wanted convict to remain untouched by France's legal statutes? Inconceivable! Javert and Valjean equal and inseparable. Two men at opposite poles of justice bound by the sacred statutes of our common motherland. These opposing possibilities tossed me this way and that like a dirty shirt in the rough hands of a washerwoman."

"At the same time, the loving arms of God embraced you, Javert."

"This incessant back-and-forth—It overwhelmed me. How had it come to pass of a sudden that both Javert and Valjean had set themselves above the Law? To open the door to a duality in which neither received punishment—To consider a scofflaw equal to or wiser than our social order? An order fought for at times against enemies on blood-soaked French soil. To permit Valjean to remain at liberty, while I, Javert, a servant of spotless record and stellar career, ate the government's bread? Utter chaos! Unending anarchy.

"Jean Valjean gave me a second chance to live and serve my country. In doing so he took my life in his unworthy hands and crushed it into a wad of garbage. In my delirium, Monsieur Madeleine appeared behind Valjean. The two figures melded in such fashion as to form one being.

"In that instant, a terrible monster penetrated my soul. Show admiration for a convict? Respect for a galley slave? I shuddered at the thought. Yet, I found no escape route to freedom... freedom from myself. In vain did I struggle to construct a path to self-respect.

Charles, I confess in my inmost heart… the sudden sublimity of an odious wretch such as Jean Valjean. A benevolent malefactor, merciful, gentle, generous. An escaped convict who returned good for evil, pardon for hatred… who chose pity over vengeance. A man who chose his own ruin rather than destroy an enemy. He spared the one who had smitten him.

I beheld him kneeling before the altar of virtue, more nearly akin to an angel than a man. In the end, solemn truth forced me to admit…"

"Admit what, Javert?"

"I had sold myself into slavery, wherein I devolved into a man no better than a monster. I confess to you, Charles, I could not tolerate living in such a manner. Better that I should—"

CHAPTER THE NINETEENTH:
TRANSCENDENT PAIN

"Charles, what I will share with you next causes me pain transcending any I experienced in my five decades of life."

"I assure you, Javert, I shall receive whatever you share with respect and compassion. Feel free to expose whatever you need to. You have arrived at a safe place."

"Thank you. My brain, once secure in its blindness, lost... transparency. Like a suddenly clouded crystal. I who never felt conflicted in mission or duty suddenly experienced—How to describe it?"

"A divided conscience?"

"Exactly. Thank you, Charles. You always have just the right words. It began this night—Do I still exist in the last night of my Earth life? It all seems so... distant."

"Javert—"

"Yes, yes, I know. The irrelevance of time and sequence. Jean Valjean dragged that dead revolutionary out of the sewer and laid him on the bank of the Seine. Hitherto, I saw myself as the wolf springing from cover in the woods to grip in my powerful jaw an unsuspecting prey. Divine Justice had gifted me with an opportunity to right my wrong. I regained mastery of my prey, a man who had fallen to the lowest depths of depravity, stealing a coin from a hardworking lad. Joining a revolution against the sovereign state of France. I vowed to see him pay dearly for his post-parole crimes. But—"

"Take this at your own pace, my brother."

"Had I in truth set him free by my independent statement, 'Go,' meaning, 'live free.' I tell you, Charles, this bundle of contradictions... it overwhelmed me in the moment and still now."

"My dear Javert, I can only imagine your suffering. We can pause here if you need to ponder the source of your confusion over this life-changing development. I can only offer a bit of kindly guidance, to assist you here and there in your spiritual discernment."

"Though I suffer, Charles, I must go on."

*　　　　*　　　　*

"Remember, Javert, you do not walk this difficult journey alone."

"For that, Charles, I offer my gratitude."

"As you know, I serve only as your divinely commissioned guide. You have my full support and, perhaps what you need even more, my presence as you proceed."

"Would you like to know what most amazed me and yes, disturbed me, about my inner warfare?"

"Indeed I would. You must mean the events that unleashed your spiral of confusion."

"Yes, that Jean Valjean should have done me, of all people, a favor. I had dedicated my life to seeing him pay for his crimes and the years he stole from our prison system. His generosity at the barricade paled before what petrified me. That I, Inspector Javert, repaid Valjean with... a favor! In that instant, the ground beneath my feet rolled and heaved.

"Alone on the banks of the Seine, I sought comprehension of my position. I deemed it wrong to deliver Jean Valjean into the grasp of the prison system. Granting him liberty bore even greater criminality on my part. The man of authority fell lower than the galley slave. The convict rose above the Law, trampled it beneath his boot. In each case, dishonor had fallen upon the previously impeccable Inspector Javert. No matter which path I chose, disgrace awaited me."

*　　　　*　　　　*

"Who can define destiny, Charles? Reflection upon the events of my final day of life tortures me. How to rectify my fall from grace?"

"Never have I encountered a more anguished spirit, Javert. Sainted mystics refer to your experience as the soul's 'dark night.'"

"A chilling metaphor."

"What you insist on calling your fall *from* grace I celebrate as your leap *into* grace."

"I fear you have made a premature assessment, one you will later retract."

"We shall see, Javert. Our God does not act according to values extant in French upper-class society."

"If a betting man, I'd wager all my chips on my cards, though in my whole life I never gambled… on anything. Some fellow officers played cards or rolled dice. Not I. Never."

"Proceed with your story, Javert."

"At the end of my internal warfare, I came to the decision I posited earlier."

"Return to Valjean's home and arrest him?"

"Despite my vacillation, no higher realm could exist beyond the sacred laws of our government, including its tribunals, its mandated sentences, and the officers who kept the peace along our precious yet often dangerous boulevards and alleyways?"

"Still you failed to find peace in your resolve."

"You have come to know me well, Charles. Too well for my comfort."

"I only know what you reveal to me and what I garner from your life story."

"An insurmountable force barred my way. Making it close to impossible to return to Rue de l' Homme Arme. As I battled against my act of unheard of leniency, one misguided conviction overwhelmed my better self. Could the life of a galley slave stand sacred before God? Impossible! Should I call an end to my pursuit? Allow Valjean to remain at liberty while I, Javert, go on earning a tainted income—How ever to recover from such a fall? Allow such abnormalities to permeate society without punishment? Cast the notorious Valjean as a living saint—equal to France's own Vincent de Paul and Benedict Joseph Labre?

"Could I wear the sacred vestments of my office, while an army of loyal policemen risked their lives each day to keep every corner of France safe from the likes of Jean Valjean? Stride into an alternate reality as if nothing of consequence had happened between us? God Almighty! This and another flood of hellish questions tormented me as I stared into the churning abyss beneath my feet.

"Only evil lurked at the end of that slippery path. Most of all, why had all this happened to me? Overnight, all virtue and diligence crumbled in the presence of that despicable man. In the end, Valjean's generosity… well, it destroyed me. How I wished he had put the pistol to my head and pulled that trigger."

"I regret the torture you endured in that moment, Javert. Impossible as it seems to you, the deepest darkness precedes the dawn."

"Except my sun never rose, nor will it for a wretched failure like me. Everything I treated as lies and folly now claimed the role of higher truth. Tell me, Charles, how does a turncoat pariah, one with TRAITOR branded on his chest, recover from such a fall? You might say, 'Move on.' I counter with, 'To what?'"

"As you have learned, Javert, I receive your revelations with compassion, admiration even."

*   *   *

"Sadly, my final judgment shall not come from you. I tell you, Charles, I shuddered at the truth of my fall from grace. I searched for an escape route but found none."

"I can only imagine the torments you suffered."

"Permit me to correct you, Charles. A man like you, a faithful, lifelong servant of our Savior, cannot possibly know the torments of a man standing paralyzed at an unmarked crossroad, still and silent."

"You speak the truth. We each bear our pain as a unique entity among all creation. Each one's sufferings belong to him and no one else who ever lived on planet Earth. Or ever will."

*   *   *

"In vain did I struggle to regain equilibrium, Charles. This night, perched on the parapet, I—How to say this? I... evolved. I saw in my tormentor a misguided but benevolent malefactor... a merciful and clement convict who returned good for evil, pardon for hatred, kindness for vengeance. He risked ruin to himself over harm to his relentless enemy. What sort of man spares the one who smote him ceaselessly without mercy? My vision so altered I saw him raised to the heights of virtue, more akin to an angel than a man."

"A remarkable testimony to your conversion of mind and heart, Javert."

"An affirmation you may soon wish to withdraw, I fear. As I sat in that reeking carriage with Valjean on our way to Rue de l'Homme Arme, the legal tiger roared within me, as never before. A score of times, I fought with an urge to fling myself at him, throttle him, giving myself the pleasure of watching him writhe beneath my boot and die right there in the carriage. The driver? He wouldn't dare turn me in. The 'false' word of a man with a reputation as a spotless defender of right order against Valjean's history of criminal wrongdoing. No question whom my superiors would believe. How satisfying to live thereafter in confidence that I had served the good of my country.

"I planned all this in silence, but as my passion boiled, I'd have sworn I spoke the words aloud. I could not proceed in this split-minded state. Yet—"

"You doubted."

"In the depths of these thoughts, an unaccustomed, alien voice addressed me, '*Would you deliver up your savior, Javert?*'"

* * *

"I rehearsed my confession to the Prefect. 'Sir, I betrayed my office in the most egregious manner, degrading both myself and my profession.'

"'How, Inspector?' the Prefect would ask with shock darting from his eyes.

"'I set a guilty man, free... a convict on the run, one Jean Valjean, known as well by a string of aliases. On my own, I allowed convict 24601 to become my benefactor.'

"In turn, I heard a deep bearlike growl in the Prefect's stern demand, 'Explain what you mean, Inspector.'

"I'd oblige him with a detailed admission of my misguided acts and unforgivable guilt. 'The leader of the insurgency, one Enjolras, assigned my execution to that same escapee. Instead, the convict permitted me to leave the barricade unharmed. His mercy has now become my... my shame. A yoke around my neck.' At least, Charles, I needed to confess that much."

"But—"

"I did not. For that one neglectful act, I merit eternal hellfire."

"What you label a 'yoke,' Javert, may instead have sealed your salvation."

"You cannot convince me to believe otherwise, Charles. God Almighty condemns all liars and cowards, foremost those sworn to speak truth to a superior. No one in history, not even Judas Iscariot, abused sacred truth as blatantly and with more unpardonable cowardice."

"Explain to me, Javert, why you think Valjean disobeyed Enjolras's order."

"A man of the cloth cannot fathom what motivates a soldier in the din and confusion of battle to make misguided decisions. I have spoken too much about Valjean. I will now focus on my own guilt. My supreme anguish derived from an inconceivable loss of certitude. I applied an axe to the roots of the Civil Code that provided me with a reason for living and a salary sufficient to maintain my frugal living mode.

"There came to me a revelation entirely distinct from legal affirmation. Hitherto, the Law provided my only standard of measurement. I no longer deserved my renowned reputation of uprightness and the advanced position of my office, one step below the Prefect himself. Most shocking to me, if you can believe this, Charles, I no longer desired to remain in my lofty position. God in heaven! How quickly and completely I lost my bearings. All because of that man's cursed kindness.

"A strange—uncomfortable—new world dawned in my soul. Kindness called for acceptance and favor in return. If you can believe this, I begged for the loss of positive conviction.

"This jumble of thoughts and emotions, forbidden since my youth for fear of becoming a copy of my wretched parents, horrified me. In the same instant, the thought of acting rightly... dazzled me."

"Javert, I praise you for your remarkable candor in sharing the warfare raging within your soul. Your detailed description of Jean Valjean's behavior calls to mind a passage from the Book of Exodus, Chapter 23, Verse 5. Perhaps you've heard it in a Sunday sermon."

"After a Saturday night of patrolling crime-ridden streets, I confess to nodding through the most animated sermons."

"It reads thusly, 'When you see the donkey of a man who hates you, falling under his load, do not pass by but help him.' Centuries later, Jesus taught, as recorded in Matthew's gospel, Chapter 5, Verses 44 to 48, 'You have heard it said: Love your neighbor but do no good to your enemy. But I tell you: love your enemies. Pray for those who persecute you, so you may become children of your Father in Heaven. For he makes his sun rise on both the wicked and the good. He gives rain to both the just and the unjust. If you love those who love you, what makes that special? Even tax collectors do as much. And if you offer friendship only to your friends, what makes that exceptional? Even pagans do as much, do they not? As for you, aim at perfection, in the same manner as your heavenly Father.'"

"Charles, I long ago rejected any such naïve and impractical standards. I consider it... dangerous, even, for a man in my profession. Imagine if you can the perils of life in our cruel world. Perhaps you prefer not to know what takes place in the dens of human iniquity I stalked and exposed during my illustrious career in service to law-abiding society.

"My life collapsed that one night in the carriage delivering young Pontmercy's dead body home to his family. Even more egregiously when I delivered Valjean to his residence, only to dismiss my driver and slink away in the shadows of night."

"Tell me again why you changed your mind so suddenly, Javert."

"I came to see that—the unthinkable words tie a noose around my throat—exceptional cases do in fact exist. A rule might prove inadequate in the presence of countering facts. Some laws... do not fit every situation. Not everything nests comfortably when measured against a particular text of the legal Code. Some happenstances might compel obedience to... yes, I now admit... a higher law.

"I acknowledged that goodness—a hitherto alien linkage of vowels and consonants—does indeed exist. An unprecedented circumstance might demand exception. I admit that an escaped convict might extend mercy to an enemy, even one such as me. Yes, justice might indeed—oh my, dare I say it?—allow good behavior among the criminal class. In concluding thus, I judged myself a coward, unworthy of the uniform I had worn seemingly since childhood.

"Peering into the blackness of the Seine, I passed judgment on myself as I would a criminal caught *in flagrante delicto*. I clasped my head in both hands, hoping somehow to survive this moral cannonade.

"I had Valjean under my foot. I *had* him! The good Lord in Heaven had gifted me, at last, with my sweetest avenging victory. How to define Valjean's greatest betrayal, his greatest sin, granting me unwanted, undeserved mercy? Forgive me, Charles, I cannot go on."

"Javert, I thank our God for never putting me in your position. My first allegiance now as always rests in Jesus Christ, whom I serve without reserve. Should a papal or episcopal mandate clearly violate my conscience, my ordination as priest demanded primary obedience to my God-given sense of right and wrong. I knew then, as I do now, where to cast my higher allegiance. I cannot experience your intense pain, but you have my pledge of brotherhood and compassion."

CHAPTER THE TWENTIETH:
HEALING A BLIND MAN

"Without consciousness of doing so, I swear it, Charles, I found myself standing on the parapet! My balance became, shall I say, disjointed. Scales fell from the eyes of my soul. In one vision, I fell into the hungry abyss swirling below me. In the other, I soared heavenward.

"For the first time—ever—I begged for light to make the better choice. Perched on the parapet, one fact dominated all else. I had committed an unpardonable infraction, shutting my eyes on an escaped convict.

"In a terrifying revelation, I saw the truth with luminous clarity. I had lived my life in a state of faithless faith, engendered by gloomy probity. That same conviction abandoned me in the dark hours following my rescue from certain death.

"Everything I had believed in… the core of my identity—It all vanished. O horrid dilemma, Charles! How could I return to my post as the same man? Worse, how to live with my newborn conviction. In that moment, I felt emptied, purged, useless, and out of joint with my past, my all-important self-identity. I fell lower than the worst criminal I ever put in chains."

*　　　*　　　*

"With all authority lying dead within me, I no longer justified my existence. 'A bronze statue of Chastisement,' my fellow officers called me, 'cast in the sacred mold of Law.' In a single instant to become aware of something within my spirit I'd held as absurd since childhood. I labeled this intruding spirit as something resembling... a heart!"

"What a blessing, Javert."

"Hold your applause, Charles. I, Inspector Javert, struck the fear of God and the Law into every man, woman, and child who found themselves in the clutches of this peerless foe of everything evil. From that lofty height to fall victim to—of all things—doubt! To descend from that mount of virtue to the level of perpetrator guilty of grave sin—"

"What sin, Javert?"

"Returning good for evil. To feel my fingers opening, my grip relaxing on the throat of my nemesis, my savior. That a codex of Law might not speak the final word. Civil society imperfect? Could error exist in legal dogma? Could authority compromise itself with vacillation? Had the immutable suffered, God forbid, a crack? I envisioned no more shameful end to a spotless career.

"How to integrate the sudden awareness that judges, after all, stand before God as mere men? That Law may err? That a tribunal might issue a... mistaken judgment? Charles, these terrifying doubts sabotaged my soul. I had no past experience of an unknown hanging over my head. Prior to that moment, I accepted authority as an unblemished surface. Then why now this dizziness in its presence?

"This unprecedented apparition of... what shall I call it? Otherness. It terrified me. As did those haunting spirits who invaded my childhood nightmares in that woman's cell. If I allowed this temptation into my life, in whom or what might I trust? How does an honest servitor of the law perform his duties when caught between canceling crimes—allowing Valjean to escape and arresting him? My brain burst from the birth pangs of... choice."

"Javert, I once faced a similar conundrum when I came into possession of a chest full of vestments and other items stolen from a neighboring diocese's cathedral. My choices? Return the damaged items to their rightful owner or use the proceeds of their sale to care for impoverished patients in our local hospital."

"So then, in truth, Charles, blind alleys do exist? And manifest themselves in the performance of one's sacred duty?"

"I wish not but yes. What you call a 'blind alley' demands the most difficult of all moral choices. One relies on the weight of pros and cons. Ultimately, on an informed conscience."

"So, Charles, a ruffian sent to prison by a jury of peers might end up in the right? Live, in fact, in the conviction of innocence?"

"It happens. More often than a man in your position might desire to acknowledge."

"Yes, I saw it myself. Touched it! Held it within the palm of my hand. In my case, there no longer existed room for denial For the first time I admitted, 'Javert, you've lost this match.' The time had come to declare Valjean the winner of our lifelong duel. My God! How to live at peace with such a conclusion?"

"You will learn, Javert. You will."

"Perched on the rail in that moment, alone and staring into the inviting waters, I allowed the argument to rage on. In my soul's dark night, this wounded warrior and once incorruptible bulldog in the service of the Law had filled himself with gut-wrenching confusion."

*   *   *

"Brother Javert, I grieve over your anguish of soul. That said, I deem your spiritual turmoil a wondrous blessing to you from Christ Jesus, who died for you a criminal's death. I rejoice in your willingness to wrestle with the widely disparate voices pulling you hither and yon."

"Charles, I dare not call what I experienced on the parapet 'willingness' to cooperate. Rather, for an instant or an hour, I cannot say which, I stepped outside my body and observed the grappling of two equal, fierce, and mighty competitors. Warring on... weary to death... neither surrendering."

"Nonetheless, Javert, I see you now with new and clearer appreciation. I suffered my own share of grappling with life and death decisions. I speak of the torment I endured during the prolonged crisis before, during, and after the death of my beloved wife. Still, my experience of standing at a crossroads moment in my life, uncertain about turning left or right—or retreating along my original path as opposed to proceeding forward in the same direction. …All this pales before the struggle you described with such sincere eloquence."

"You misplace your well-intended conclusions, dear friend Charles. Nothing can change the final outcome of the drama I once called my life… my fate. You have yet to hear the final, defining moments that set me on the highway to Hell. I know the Ten Commandments. I can recite them from memory. The Eighth Commandment condemns me for all eternity for 'bearing false witness'—to myself. Though I wish my destiny otherwise, our just God, not you, shall render final judgment."

"True, Javert. Judgment lies beyond the pale of my power and duties. For that I thank the good Lord."

*   *   *

"The only path to life I saw following my release of Valjean required me to lie to my superior—and live that lie for the rest of my tarnished life. How endure each guilt-ridden day knowing that, beneath my uniform and medals, there existed a man of flesh, one no better than the criminals I arrested? How long before I again found reason to look the other way rather than handcuff and jail a youth I caught stealing a few melons to bring home to a malnourished mother and siblings? Or apples by a dolt like Champmathieu?

"Instead, I chose the coward's way out. There you have it, Charles. Not even you can alter or prevent my final judgment. As a young officer, I envisioned dying in the line of duty. I expected my God to welcome me into the kingdom of heaven. Now, I shall never hear those final words of Jesus—"

"'Come, blessed of my Father, inherit the kingdom prepared for you from the foundation of the world,' Matthew 25."

"Exactly. That night at the Seine, I forfeited forever the eternal company of my Divine Judge."

"What alternate verdict do you expect at your sentencing, Javert?"

"In that same parable, if I recall correctly, the Judge proclaims the opposite outcome to those unworthy souls who, like me, failed their test. 'Depart from me, accursed ones, into the everlasting fire prepared for Satan and his angels.' You see, Charles, despite your encouragement, our Divine Judge has sealed my fate."

CHAPTER THE TWENTY-FIRST:
EVOLUTION

"So, do we now approach the final scene in your life review, Javert?"

"We do indeed."

"I detect a note of sorrow, with an upsetting undercurrent of bitterness, aimed more at yourself than Jean Valjean."

"Most astute, Charles. A true reader of souls."

"Please know this, my brother, I bear your sorrow in my spirit. I bear your regret, and—yes—even your seething anger and self-hatred."

"I bear my burden… alone."

"What happened, Javert, after this prolonged bout with your unknown angel?"

*   *   *

"I stepped down from the parapet onto the quay and stood spine-erect for the second time since granting Jean Valjean his freedom. I set off in the direction of the stationhouse on the Place du Chatelet. Arriving after midnight, I saw through the window a sergeant of police but hesitated not a second before entering.

"Though well known, I flashed my new identity card and seated myself at a table on which a single candle had already burned to half its original size. On the table lay a pen, a leaden inkstand, and blank sheets of paper, in the event an officer needed to write a report or leave orders for the next patrol. These materials exist in all prefectures.

"Lest I should yield to insistent second thoughts, I snatched the pen with a firm grip. Drawing a sheet of paper close, I wrote the following to my superior officer…

A Few Observations For The Good of the Service.

I beg Monsieur le Prefect to cast his eyes on these few pages.

First: According to current practice, upon arriving at the station prisoners must remove their shoes and stand barefoot on the flagstone floors while undergoing a search and log in. In winter months, many become ill on their way to prison. This entails unnecessary medical expenses for the prefecture. This practice must stop.

Second: When transporting individuals from one distance to another, keeping track of a man with relays of single agents may serve well in a case of lesser consequence. For situations demanding greater security, I recommend employment of two-agent teams. This change eliminates the possibility of the guards losing sight of each other, should one officer, for any cause, find himself unable continue. A second officer stands ready to step in thus maintaining the prisoner's secure supervision.

Third: The women's Prison of the Madelonettes currently forbids prisoners to have a chair. On occasions when a prisoner requires one, some guards demand payment for the 'privilege' of sitting in it! This unjust practice must cease.

Fourth: Also at the Madelonettes, the cell door's canteen drawer has only two bars. This allows the canteen woman space to touch a prisoner's hand, leading to abuses. Example: passing contraband notes and parcels.

Fifth: In Madame Henry, we have an honest woman. She keeps a neat canteen. However, entrusting a woman to guard high-risk inmates presents an unnecessary danger. This shameful behavior mars the Conciergerie of a great civilization.

Sixth: Prisoners called 'barkers' force other prisoners to pay them two sous for a legitimate summons to the parlor. We must no longer tolerate this form of extortion.

Seventh: In the workshops, guards charge ten sous—yes, ten!—for a broken thread. This constitutes an abuse when the cloth clearly reveals no diminishment of its usefulness.

Eighth: Visitors to the juvenile lockup La Force at Sainte-Marie-l'Egyptienne must pass through the boys' court on the way to the parlor. This needless endangerment of our citizens demands correction.

Ninth: Every day, in the courtyard of the prefecture, gendarmes exchange information gleaned from magistrates' private interrogations of prisoners. Another grave disorder. They must swear not to repeat what they hear in the examination room.

*　　　*　　　*

"I wrote these lines, Charles, with utmost care and, I admit, with unaccustomed serenity of spirit, taking care not to omit a single comma or period. Every 'i' dotted, every 't' crossed. The intensity of my grip on the pen caused the paper at times to screech. Below the last line I added my signature and rank.

JAVERT, Inspector of the 1st Class
The Post of the Place du Chatelet
June 7th, 1832, one o'clock in the morning

"I dried the fresh ink and folded the paper in thirds, slid it into an envelope and sealed it. In bold strokes I wrote, '*NOTE FOR THE PREFECT.*'

"Leaving the document on the table, I rose and exited the prefecture. I then traversed the Place du Chatelet diagonally. I found myself at the quay with my feet planted on the precise paving-stone as before—as if I had not marched back to the precinct at all.

"It felt to me a… sepulchral moment. In my absence, rain showers had ceased, yielding to a ceiling of clouds that darkened the earlier moonlight, like the closing of a coffin lid. A misty blanket obscured the two squared towers of Notre Dame. At that hour, pedestrian and coach travel vanished from the streets and quays. Nary a light burned anywhere in nearby buildings and residences. Outlines of the Seine's bridges stood shapeless, fading from view one beyond the other.

"Summer rains had swollen the river, increasing its danger for anyone foolhardy enough to enter its death trap. The spot where I leaned placed me precisely over the shadowed rapids, perpendicular to that invisible spiral. I bent my head to gaze into the blackened swirl, hearing but not seeing.

"Out of that bleakness a diabolical breath rose from the abyss. The river morphed into a chorus of garbled whisperings. Suddenly, my awe turned to terror. I remained motionless for several minutes, gazing into the hollow shadow.

"All at once, without recollection of having made a decision to do so, I removed my hat and dropped it carefully to the ground. ...I stepped onto the parapet. ...A moment later, I stood at military attention, then bent forward toward the unseen menace below.

"Sensing the risk of losing my balance, I stood erect once more. Neither thought nor sound entered my consciousness. Even the whirling waters below fell silent. Oblivious to the open jaws lying in wait... I stepped into the darkness."

"And your arrival here in Afterlife became your next awake and conscious moment?"

"Not precisely, Charles."

"Go on."

"A stranger approached me. ...You. Out of nowhere, you appeared to me!"

"True. My Lord and Master summoned me to welcome you to this other side of Life. An assignment I delight in. You see now for yourself that death does not exist as a permanent fate but as a passageway. One's life on planet Earth springs into a new state of being we refer to here as Afterlife."

"Not likely, I fear, Charles. Not likely at all. With great sensitivity, Charles, you have fulfilled your difficult mission to accompany me through this reluctant life-review. For that, I thank you. I opened my Hell-bound spirit to you—as I had to no one ever before. Yet you do not condemn me. Why?"

"I serve only to—"

"Yes, I know, 'to welcome and guide.' You have served me well, my gentle guide. Surely, you cannot have gained the slightest pleasure from walking me back through my misguided life. You know me now as I allowed no other. I see more clearly now than I ever did in Earth life."

"Javert, I give thanks to our good and merciful Lord for choosing me to accompany you on this journey. I also thank you, my friend, for your spiritual and moral honesty."

"On the other side, I called no man or woman 'friend.'"

"Never? Why?"

"They might one day betray my trust."

"Your admission grieves me, Javert. I thank you all the more for sharing your darkest, most guarded secrets. Your honesty—It humbles me."

"I stand ready for the Gates of Hell to swallow me. Soon, I hope."

"I shall report to our merciful Christ that I have witnessed the sincere and complete confession of your soul's dark inner journey. But for now, Javert, the time has come for us to part."

"Of course. Our destinies point in opposite directions."

"I shall miss you, brother Javert. Farewell. I pray we meet again."

CHAPTER THE TWENTY-SECOND:
DARKNESS TO LIGHT

Alone again.

How can you abandon me, Charles? Leave me here…? Why do I experience a sudden need for—? What to call it even? Unaccustomed… companionship… dare I say friendship? Alas! Have I discovered the true meaning of Hell? Not fire, as I believed, but solitude. Emptiness. Terrifying thoughts rush to mind. To live with myself in everlasting… aloneness. The very condition I craved on Earth I now dread more than anything. Only now do I comprehend the torture of solitary confinement. How many men and women did I gleefully cast into that abyss?

Why this change? On Earth I never craved companionship. I needed only myself—sought the company of no other, male or female. Not even a pet. I prided myself on unmatched skills and virtues of my profession… self-sufficiency… self-discipline. Emphasis always on the 'Self.' I sought these virtues as highest among the categories of earthly excellence.

I allowed no one to enter—even approach—my inner sanctum, let alone trespass into the most private chamber of my spirit. Never did I experience the need or desire to share my life, not as a young man, never in the prime of my career. Why? Not out of commitment to consecrated chastity like a cloistered religious. My true, unspoken reason? I lived in perpetual shame of my unsavory entry into life on Earth. Not once in my impeccable career did I permit anyone to peer beyond the medals and uniform I wore with pride and distinction.

I foresaw my place in eternity as a private abode high among heaven's ranks. I expected to enjoy forever the life of a holy hermit basking in the glory of the Beatific Vision.

Inexplicably, I now crave the companionship of my gentle guide, Charles Francois Myriel. I understood our need to part once I strode through Hell's gates into the furnace that never exhausts its punishing fuel—or now into the torture chamber of eternal solitary confinement.

I blame the Renaissance masters who mistakenly portrayed Hell as eternal flames and the company of devils and other corrupt men and women whose lives of sin and degradation cast them there. Instead, I now face a failed soul's most unbearable fate.

Someone approaches.

*　　　　　*　　　　　*

"Javert!"

These two syllables rise above the harmonious chanting of, I suspect, devils masquerading as angels.

"Who calls?"

"Jesus, the Risen Christ, who died for you. Now, I have come for you, Javert."

"You cannot fool me, Satan. Have you no shame? You come in the person of God's Son, only to commit me to the eternal silence reserved for me. In Inspector Javert you have met your match."

"Brother Javert, you cannot serve as ultimate judge of your own life."

"Liar! I spent a lifetime dealing with slime like you. I know your tricks. Take me, though I dread my fate. Justice demands that I accept the punishment due for my wasted life. Show me the way to my solitary lair of eternal nothingness."

"Listen closely, Javert. I saw you eighteen centuries ago in Earth time. I lay wounded on a lonely road as you passed by. You judged me unworthy of your attention, let alone any trace of compassion."

"You... saw me? Another lie! Have you no shame? No end to your trickery?"

"At other times, I appeared at your door hungry, but you offered me nothing to eat. I thirsted… you offered not a single drop of cool water to quench my thirst. In my nakedness, you—dressed in your immaculate uniform bedecked with impressive medals—offered neither blanket nor garment to cover me."

"Another lie!"

"When I hoisted the sins of the world on my back, you led the Roman guards assigned to prod me on toward Calvary. You lashed me repeatedly with your leather whip as one would a stubborn beast of burden. Thrice I fell under my load. Though strong and fit, you offered no aid. When I dragged my torn flesh up the hill of Calvary, you ripped the seamless, blood-soaked garment from my back, reopening clotted stripes. Through my dimming eyes I watched you cavalierly cast lots even for that spoiled souvenir."

"Hold! You must mistake me for someone else, sir. I lived a blameless life… with but one damning exception."

"Over the din of wailing women, my dearest mother among them, you mocked me: 'Look at yourself, Jesus of Nazareth! Do you persist in claiming the ridiculous title Pontius Pilate ordered me to post above your head? Jesus of Nazareth, King of the Jews. Hah! A king without subjects willing to shed a drop of their own blood to save you.'"

"I said no such thing, you artful deceiver!"

"Javert, you mocked me further with these hateful words, 'If you wear the crown of a king, call upon your army. Does no one come to your aid but these mewling women and that dumb-struck youth? Who among them has the strength to pull the nails from your hands or stop the bleeding from your thorny crown!'"

"Silence, master of deceit!"

"Javert, I listened as you shouted over the cries of those crucified on my left and right, 'If you persist in proclaiming yourself Son of God, show your power. Come down from that cross. Now. Before you exhale your final breath.'"

"Listen, Satan—Or whoever you are. I have proof of your lies and command you to confess the error in your accusation. I did not exist until a whoring woman birthed me in the year of Our Lord 1780. Nearly two millennia after the events you describe in such graphic terms. Thus, I declare you mistaken. I served both State and Church with great distinction to the moment of my sole misguided step."

"Your past remains just that, Javert. In the past. You left both title, rank, and résumé on the parapet, the night you—"

"Why must you insist on reminding me? Had I not yielded to the fatal error of releasing a lifelong criminal from my custody, I might have salvaged my career, my life… restored my peerless reputation. My eternal salvation."

"Tell me about your 'fatal error,' as you call it."

"I allowed a wanted criminal—one Jean Valjean—to return that young lawyer and fellow insurrectionist to his home for burial. And…"

"Say it, Javert."

"I compounded my betrayal of duty by freeing my sworn enemy."

"Yes, my faithful servant, Jean Valjean."

"So you know him, Satan. No surprise. He did not merit a second chance at life. The day will come when he joins me here in Hell. Had I returned to the station house and resumed my position as second in command of the Paris Prefecture no one would have dared question my whereabouts that evening or my decisions. Nor did anyone deserve a detailed account of my behavior at the barricade."

"Javert, do you install yourself then as final arbiter and judge of your behavior?"

"I do, indeed, Satan, you imposter in sheep's clothing. Who are you to question my authority? To question my qualifications or my judgment? I defended without peer all that proved right and good in French society… until, that is, I committed my solitary crime. I confided all this to Bishop Charles, my guide. Now, I pass judgment on myself. Guilty on all counts! My sentence? Eternity in the silence of Hell. Court dismissed!"

"On your final declaration, Javert, we both agree. Guilty indeed. Fortunately for you and all who spend their Earth life indulging in evil deeds of every variety, there exists a higher court."

"Do you speak of a tribunal beyond my acknowledged guilt and self-pronounced sentence?"

"Infinitely higher than your court of one. Now, Javert, open wide the eyes and ears of your soul. Peer deeper into truth than your prideful conviction has allowed you. What do you see?"

*   *   *

"Light.

"Intense brightness.

"I see… myself as I never have before."

"What else do you see?"

"I see… hope."

"What do you hear."

"Music! An angelic choir."

A massive throng of souls approach. Hostile or benevolent I do not know. By instinct and training, I prepare myself to defend against an impending attack. Instead, I find myself wrapped in, of all things… Love. A word and state I shunned as a distraction from my lifelong mission to serve God by keeping civil order amid the criminal classes, society's deepest, most ungodly underworld.

An unknown but familiar man and woman lead a joyous throng of welcomers. I cannot believe what I see, but I must. The very ones who rejected me at birth and failed to endow me with a proper saint's name. That never-seen but hated stranger, my… father.

Alongside him my mother, beaming, offering the love I longed for from birth—but never knew. And therefore never bestowed upon anyone else. No one!

My first, instinctive act, had I encountered either of them alive and free on Earth? Handcuff and drag them by the hair to the nearest lockup. How often in life I played out that scenario both in dreams and waking fantasies. Each repetition ended with vile castigation for depriving me of the parental love I craved but never knew.

It stuns me now to encounter them here, together… to see their… joy… their genuine love… for me! For each other! I relish their welcoming embrace of the man-child they abandoned in swaddling clothes at the doorstep of France's penal system. And now? An unthinkable reunion as—the words balk at expression—

my... family. They invite me into their circle of love. We... we embrace to the accompaniment of a chorus of angelic hosts.

*   *   *

Such, then... the story of my life.
Rewritten.

AFTERWORD

I offer my special gratitude to my prereaders, whose spot-on comments, suggestions, and encouragement I appreciated and drew upon.

Steve Physioc, author of *The Walls of Lucca* (2018) and *Above the Walls* (2019), two wonderful novels about a family of winegrowers in Italy from the end of World War I through World War II. Steve's third novel, *Walks With the Wind* (2021) features the gripping story of a young American Indian, who foregoes a career in baseball to become a tracker in Afghanistan. Next in the works, a sequel to *Walks with the Wind*. When Steve isn't writing, he broadcasts the Kansas City Royals' baseball games on radio and TV. You can learn more about Steve at *stevephysioc.com*.

James Farmer, author of *Celluloid Wings, Broken Wings,* and *America's Pioneer Aces.* His novel-in-progress, *Manna Rains*, brings to vivid life the Allied Forces food drop to starving Netherlanders near the end of World War II.

James Gallagher, whose theological knowledge and keen insight I sought and am grateful for. Thanks also to Honey O'Leary who, like Jim, brought her unique spiritual depth that kept me on track through the early drafts of *Inspector Javert*.

Andrei, Natalie, and Natasha Middleton encouraged me and offered greatly appreciated suggestions.

Andrew Benzie designed the stunning cover and interior design for this book.

*   *   *

As I considered writing *Inspector Javert*, I wondered if Victor Hugo publicly addressed the issue of his legendary policeman's ascendance to light.

I searched for justification within the text of *Les Misérables* that Javert might have made a prior-to-death conversion. Hugo answered my question near the end of the 1,200-plus page novel. In an authorial aside buried deep within Jean Valjean, Book the First, Chapter XX, we read:

> *"The book which the reader has before his eyes is, from one end to the other, in its whole and in its details, whatever may be the intermissions, the exceptions or the defaults, the march from evil to good, from injustice to justice, from the false to the true, from night to day, from appetite to conscience, from rottenness to life, from brutality to duty, from Hell to Heaven, from nothingness to God. Starting point: matter; goal: the soul. Hydra at the beginning, angel at the end."*

With this discovery, I received permission from the master storyteller himself to retell the story of his unforgettable Inspector Javert's life, death, and passage to eternity.

It also occurred to me in writing this version of Inspector Javert's life that Hugo might have had Saul of Tarsus (St. Paul the Apostle) in mind as the prototype for Javert. In the years prior to his conversion to Christianity, Saul despised that new offshoot of Judaism, the heretical followers of Jesus of Nazareth. The comparison leaps out. Saul obtained permission from the Jewish high priest to arrest every so-called Messiah follower. And to execute, if necessary, those who refused to recant. Saul carried out his mission with the same single-minded zeal that drove Hugo's antihero. Without conscious reflection, Javert comported himself as France's Saul of Tarsus.

VICTOR HUGO IN HIS OWN WORDS: ON GOD AND RELIGION

Source: Wikipedia (*abridged*)

Victor Hugo's religious views changed radically over the course of his life. In his youth and under the influence of his mother, he identified as a Roman Catholic and professed respect for Church hierarchy and authority. From there he became a non-practicing Catholic and increasingly expressed his anti-Catholic and anticlerical views.

He frequented a reader of spirits during his exile to Guernsey, participating in many séances conducted by Madame Delphine de Girardin. In his later years, he settled into a rationalist deism similar to that espoused by Voltaire.

A census taker asked Hugo in 1872 if he was a Catholic. He replied, "No. A Freethinker." After 1872, Hugo never lost his antipathy towards the Catholic Church. He felt the Church was indifferent to the plight of the working class under the oppression of the monarchy. Perhaps the frequency with which his work appeared on the Church's list of banned writings also upset him (who wouldn't be?). Hugo counted 740 attacks on *Les Misérables* in the Catholic press! When Hugo's sons, Charles and François-Victor, died, he insisted that they be buried without a crucifix or a priest. In his will, he made the same stipulation about his own death and funeral.

Yet he believed in life after death and prayed every single morning and night, convinced, as he wrote in his novel, *The Man Who Laughs*, "Thanksgiving has wings and flies to its right destination. Your prayer knows its way better than you do."

Hugo's rationalism can be found in poems such as *Torquemada* (1869, about religious fanaticism), *The Pope* (1878, his anticlericalism), *Religions and Religion* (1880, denying the usefulness of churches) and published posthumously, *The End of Satan* (1886) and *God* (1891) in which he represents Christianity as a griffin and rationalism as an angel.

He wrote:

"I feel in myself the future life. I am like a forest cut down more than once. New shoots sprout, stronger and livelier than ever. I am rising, I know, toward the endless sky. Sunshine on my head. Earth gave me its generous sap. Heaven now lights my way with the brilliant reflection of unknown worlds."

ABOUT THE AUTHOR

I identify as a confessed and unabashed Hugophile.

A native of the beautiful Southern California beach city, Santa Monica, I now reside in the San Francisco East Bay Area. I began my "career" in the arts at the age of seven, along with my sister, Natalie. We did (non-speaking) bit parts in movies requiring "Italian-looking kids." I should be honest about Natalie's sole speaking part in the "Hunchback of Notre Dame." She ran down a street with a mob screaming, "The hunchback is coming!" Natalie later used her magnificent coloratura voice to pursue a career in grand opera. Our talented younger sister, Toni, has sung and acted with Los Angeles area theater groups.

By my teens, I had veered onto a different road in academics and spirituality. Over the years, I have done a great deal of writing and teaching (mostly on Christian themes). I didn't get the book-length bug until my forties. Once the muse struck, I couldn't stop and have now written sixteen books, both fiction and nonfiction published through commercial and independent publishing channels. In addition to my love for Les Mis, my interest and topics range from biblical themes… to the arts… to steamy romance novels and poetry.

I invite you to visit my *Les Misérables* blog at:
wisdomoflesmiserables.blogspot.com

You can also find me on Facebook at:
AlfredJGarrottoAuthor. I hope you will drop by.

Also by Alfred J. Garrotto

Wisdom of Les Misérables Trilogy
Book 1
Lessons from the Heart of Jean Valjean
(nonfiction)
Book 2
Bishop Myriel: In His Own Words
(fiction)

Caribbean Tremors Trilogy
A love Forbidden
Finding Isabella
I'll Paint a Sun

There's More…
Circles of Stone
Down a Narrow Alley
The Saint of Florenville

The Soul of Art

Made in the USA
Middletown, DE
22 December 2021

56752648R00102